PEEK-A-BOO, I GUT YOU!

Longarm dipped a thumb and forefinger into the vest pocket where he kept his matches. He brought out a sulfur-tipped lucifer and used a thumbnail to snap it afire.

The result was somewhat more than he anticipated.

No sooner had the flame burst alive, surrounding him with a glare of yellow light, than he heard a roar of suprise—definitely a man's deep voice—and half heard, half saw a bulky form launching itself from a few feet to Longarm's left . . .

TABOR EVANS

LONGARM

AND THE
SHIVAREE RIDERS

JOVE BOOKS, NEW YORK

LONGARM AND THE SHIVAREE RIDERS

A Jove Book / published by arrangement with
the author

PRINTING HISTORY
Jove edition / October 1995

ISBN: 0-515-11730-7

A JOVE BOOK®
Jove Books are published by The Berkley Publishing Group,
200 Madison Avenue, New York, New York 10016.
JOVE and the "J" design are trademarks
belonging to Jove Publications, Inc.

PRINTED IN THE UNITED STATES OF AMERICA

10 9 8 7 6 5 4 3 2 1

LONGARM

AND THE
SHIVAREE RIDERS

Chapter 1

Custis Long dipped his chin and cupped his hands, shielding the flare of the lucifer flame from the breeze and dropping the tip of his slender cheroot to the fire. He concentrated on lighting the cigar and quite honestly was not paying enough attention to his surroundings as he stepped off the curb to cross Colfax Avenue in Denver's busy government district.

He damn near walked into the side of a passing coach. That was bad enough. But what was infinitely worse—worse considering the fact that the coach did miss him, if only by inches—was that the back right wheel of the rig dropped into a pothole at just that same moment. And at this early springtime of year every pothole for miles around was filled with mud and melt and mess. Brown, viscous, sloppy stuff that looked like shit. And indeed might have been. Some of it anyway.

Predictably, the splatter of brown goo sprayed quite perfectly onto Longarm's trousers from mid-shin downward, coating cloth and boots alike with cold, slimy muck.

"Damn you," he shouted as he hopped backward too late, the heel of his left boot catching on the curb and almost sending him flying onto the sidewalk on his butt.

"Dammit," he blurted again, this time glaring at the back end of the light coach.

1

The vehicle, oddly, came to a hurried stop and the driver tugged at the mouths of the pair of handsomely matched grays pulling the rig. They bowed their necks prettily and, with quick, mincing steps, backed the coach in a perfectly straight line until it was once again beside Longarm. But at a standstill this time.

For a moment Longarm thought perhaps the driver of the vehicle wanted a brawl. But hell, he hadn't yelled out anything personal. Just an involuntary yelp of complaint or two. That's all it had been.

Then he smiled and realized it was not the driver's idea to come back.

A woman—a downright handsome woman at that—was peering out the coach window at him. Closely. As if inspecting him.

"You," she said.

"Yes, ma'am."

"I've gotten your pant legs filthy, haven't I?"

"The mud did, yes," he agreed.

"But it was my fault, was it not?"

"Was it now?" He smiled. Couldn't much help smiling. This was one mighty fine-looking female. She was no youngster—now that was true. Forty, he guessed. Or even a few years older than that. But well maintained. She was wearing makeup although so skillfully applied it was not at all obvious. Just a trace here and a brushstroke there to emphasize the good features nature already gave her. And as well to minimize the wear and tear the years had provided. Nice though. Altogether nice. A hairstyle that likely cost enough to feed a working-man's family for a month and a half. A dress—he could only see her from the shoulders upward but did not need to examine the whole to realize the quality of what was before him—that was elegant and expensive. The figure contained within that dress he could only guess at, but the face was fine enough. High cheekbones. Full lips. Large, expressive eyes. And a long, slim, elegant neck.

Prime, he judged. Damn sure prime female. Rich and beautiful and therefore almost certainly married. Nevertheless a man couldn't deny the obvious. And the obvious was that this here was quite a woman.

And she in her turn seemed to be busy giving him a very similar assessment, her gaze roving boldly up and down him as he stood there beside her coach.

Well, he wasn't ashamed of what she saw. Wasn't all that impressed by it either if the truth be known, but more than a few women claimed to like what they saw when they looked at him. And if he did not completely understand their reaction, he certainly was not inclined to object to it.

A tall man, Custis Long stood some inches over six feet. He was possessed of wide, powerful shoulders but with a narrow waist and the washboard belly of the longtime horseman. He had a rugged, almost craggy face deeply tanned by years of exposure to wind and weather, and there were deep furrows spread out from the corners of his brown eyes.

He was, in fact, something of a study in brown. Brown tanned flesh, brown hair, a large but tidily groomed brown mustache, low crowned brown Stetson hat, brown tweed coat and brown corduroy trousers—spattered at the moment with brown mud—and a light-brown calfskin vest across the front of which dangled a gold watch chain.

His cavalry boots, on the other hand, were black, as was the gun belt that held a double-action, .44-40 caliber Colt's patent revolver in a crossdraw rig high on his belly just to the left of his middle.

There was a look of quiet competence about him. Generally, his appearance and bearing allowed other men to admire him without jealousy while women tended often to become moist and weak-kneed in his company.

And quite frankly he would not mind at all if this most handsome blonde woman felt that self-same way.

With that in mind he touched the brim of his hat and moved a step closer to the coach that had only moments earlier fouled both his trousers and his mood. The mud might still be on his britches, but his mood was right sunny again, thank you. He smiled and raised an eyebrow.

"Do you want me to pay you for the damage done?" the woman asked.

Longarm nodded solemnly. "Sounds like a fine idea."

"How much do you want then?"

"Oh, 'bout four hours," he mused aloud, pursing his lips and staring off toward the sky as if in deep thought. After a bit he nodded in affirmation and said, "Yeah, I'd say four hours should do it. Or a bit longer. What do you think?"

"Four hours?"

"O' your time. Over dinner mayhap. That sound fair t' you, ma'am?"

She laughed, crows-feet showing beside her eyes and mouth when she did so but the genuineness of her pleasure negating that and making her all the prettier when she laughed. "Are you asking me to dinner, sir? And we not even knowing one another?"

"Yes, ma'am, that's pretty much what I'm doing, all right."

"I don't even know your name. Nor you mine."

He grinned. "I don't know how you feel about it, but that kind adds t' my interest in the deal. Beautiful lady o' mystery, appearing outa nowhere an' disappearing just like she came. Even if you agree t' pay what I demand I won't know will you actually show up or not. Not until tonight at, say, eight o'clock?"

"Eight, is it?"

"Ayuh. At Donallo's Chop House. Do you know it?"

"I know it."

"Dominick Donallo keeps a private suite upstairs for special guests."

"That I did not know, sir."

"I'll be in that room tonight at eight. Me, mayhap a bottle of champagne. Roast quail, I think, with wild rice dressing." He smiled. "And whatever else sounds good."

"Eight o'clock?"

"Uh-huh."

4

She smiled. And did not answer. Not exactly.

"Albert," she called.

"Yes, ma'am," the driver answered from the box high up and in front of the coach.

"You may drive on now, thank you."

"Yes, ma'am." The driver took up a light contact with the mouths of his team and softly clucked to them. The grays leaned into their harness, and the coach rolled forward.

Longarm's last impression was of the woman—whose name he did not yet know—sending a secretive cat-smile at him as the vehicle pulled on down Colfax in the direction of the distant, gold-domed capitol building.

Chapter 2

"You're late," Henry accused as Longarm ambled into the office of the United States Marshal for the Denver District, U.S. Justice Department, located in the Federal Building close to the Mint on Colfax Avenue.

"You'd reckon it was worth it if you knew the reason," Longarm responded, thinking of the lady in the coach. Eight P.M. it would be, b'damn. Upstairs at Dominick's place. He was looking forward to it. And then afterward . . . well, who knew what all could happen afterward. He removed his Stetson and hung it on a bare arm of the coatrack standing in the corner.

"You might think it worthwhile," Henry countered, "but the boss is in a positively foul mood. And I think you have something to do with it."

"Me? Dammit, Henry, this time I'm innocent. I swear. I haven't done the least thing out of line. Not for weeks and weeks." Longarm grinned at the marshal's office clerk and added a wink for good measure. "Something close t' that long anyhow."

"I'm serious, Longarm. I haven't seen him this upset since . . . I can't remember how long."

This time Longarm frowned. "Hey, I'm serious too. I really

haven't done anything he should be mad at me about. Honest."

"Be that as it may, Longarm, he said he wanted to see you as soon as you came in."

"C'mon in with me then, Henry. You can hold him back if he goes for m' throat."

That elicited a hint of smile from the slightly built, bespectacled fellow behind the desk, and Henry motioned for Longarm to proceed into Marshal William Vail's inner office. Henry did not, however, choose to join Longarm and the marshal in there.

"You wanted t' see me, Billy?" Longarm asked from the doorway.

"I do," said the balding peace officer—peace-office administrator was closer to the truth of that—from the far side of the room. "Close the door behind you and have a seat."

"Yes, sir." Henry's opinion seemed right well-founded, Longarm decided. There was nothing light or pleasant in Billy's expression this morning. Longarm did as he was told and sat gingerly on the front few inches of a straight-backed chair before the marshal's big desk. His normal posture was lax and casual. But not today. That, he figured, would be as good as asking for Billy to let fly with whatever bees were swarming in his bonnet.

Vail, who was getting a bit of a belly on him now that his days were spent largely riding a chair instead of being out ahorseback in active pursuit of wanted felons, paced the length of the room a few times in silence before taking his own much more comfortable seat at the desk.

He spun the swivel chair around so that he was facing away from Longarm and sat like that for several long moments before he turned back around and gave his top deputy a long, slow stare that was barely short of being a glare of disapproval.

"Are you acquainted with the Attorney General of the United States of America, Deputy Long?" It seemed a damned odd question. And there was something in the tone of voice . . . Longarm couldn't quite put a finger on it. But there was something a trifle out of the ordinary there.

"If you mean do I know who I work for, well o' course I do. But if you mean am I personally acquainted with the gentleman, then no, I don't recollect that I've ever met him."

"And how would he be acquainted with you, Deputy?" Vail returned.

Longarm could only shrug. "I can't see as he should be, boss. I mean, I s'pose I'd be mentioned in some reports and such. But that'd all be routine stuff. I can't think of anything more'n that." He hesitated. Then asked the obvious. "Why, d'you ask?"

The marshal frowned. And pulled a slip of flimsy memo paper out of a desk drawer. He consulted it for a moment before he spoke. "This reached me late yesterday afternoon. I would have discussed it with you sooner except I wanted to, um, confirm it . . . so to speak . . . with the United States attorney for this district before I acted on the, uh, request. Do you have any knowledge about it? Prior knowledge, that is?"

"Billy, I got no idea in th world what it is on that paper that's graveling your backside."

"Nothing is, as you put it, 'graveling' me, Deputy."

"Yes, sir. Sorry." Nothing chewing on him? Huh! Who the hell did Billy think he was fooling with that one? Not that this seemed a sensible time to mention it. But Mrs. Long's baby boy Custis hadn't been born yesterday. Not quite. "Might be I could tell you better if I knew what it was you was talking about," Longarm suggested.

Billy turned the paper around and slid it across the bare, polished surface of his desk. Longarm picked it up and gave it a quick look-see.

Then he frowned too.

"Addington, Texas? I never heard of it, Billy. Nor of this Norman Colton."

"Addington is on the Neches River between Nacogdoches and Crockett. I know because I looked it up. Does that do anything to jog your memory?"

8

"No, sir. Sorry."

"And Colton was postmaster there." It was obviously intended as a question, never mind that it wasn't posed as one. Longarm took time to give it some careful thought, then shook his head.

"I still never heard of neither the town nor the person, Billy. I'm sure of it."

The marshal's frown did not change in the slightest. "The request for your services that you see there over the signature of the U.S. attorney for this district came to me direct from the attorney general. Asking for you, Deputy. By name. And at once."

"Billy, I got no earthly idea why somebody that's got no cause ever to've heard o' me would be wanting me sent t' some place that I never heard of t' look into the murder of a postmaster I never heard of neither."

"This assignment was not your idea then?"

"Hell no."

"And you have no idea what might be going on behind my back in this matter?"

"None, boss. Really."

"I don't like it when people, in particular when they are people with political ties and political dealings, interfere with my office. This matter is not within our normal jurisdiction, as you well know. And while you have had a certain rapport in the past when dealing with Texas Rangers, Long, this does not involve them. This is purely a federal matter insofar as it appears here. But not *our* federal matter. So why am I being asked . . . no, that isn't true at all . . . why am I being *ordered* to relinquish one of my men on an independent assignment? Eh?"

"I wish I had an answer for you, Billy, but I damn sure don't." And that, by damn, was the purantee truth if ever he spoke it.

"As I mentioned earlier, I have already spoken with the United States attorney about this order from Washington. He professes to know no more about it than I do or than you say

9

you do. The bottom line, Long, is that I seem to have no choice about it. I am instructed to send you to Addington, Texas, at the earliest possible moment. You are to take the first available transportation and once there you are to investigate the death of one Norman Albert Colton, postmaster and presumably therefore a political appointee within the Attorney General's affiliated party, and you are to take whatever action you deem appropriate at the conclusion of your investigation. Is that clear, Deputy?''

''Only on the surface o' things, Billy. But then I expect you know that even better'n I do. If you know what I mean.''

The marshal grunted. And scowled. ''There is an eastbound passenger train due out of Denver at 11:19 this morning, Long. I expect you to be on it.''

''Yes, sir.''

Longarm was halfway to the door before he remembered that he had a date at eight tonight.

And no way to tell a lady whose name he did not know just why he would not be there to meet her.

Damn it anyway.

But this did not seem a good day to suggest to Marshal Billy Vail that duty should wait until Custis Long's love life was satisfied.

Not if he wanted to keep on carrying a deputy marshal's badge.

He headed for Henry's desk to pick up some travel-and-expense vouchers for the long and difficult journey down to Texas. Addington, Texas. Wherever the hell that was.

Chapter 3

Smack in the middle of the world's ugliest damned cotton patch, that's where Addington, Texas, was. Well, cotton and other stuff. Bits of row-crop bare ground scattered here and there amid thick, vine-strangled forest. Mostly cotton in the tiny fields but plenty of subsistence gardens too—folks growing a few stalks of corn here or a few hills of beans and squash and pumpkin there. It seemed the people in this area scratched out a hard living by looking to cotton for a little cash and to their gardens to eat out of.

This was definitely not the sort of country Longarm was used to. In the wide-open West, including most of Texas, a man could strain his eyes for trying to see to a far-off horizon. Here, with greenery crowding in on all sides, a man could pretty well throw a stone to the end of his vision.

And this was much older country than Longarm was used to as well.

Even as large a city as Denver was only a few years old, and many of the civic leaders had gotten their start as virtual pioneers. In Colorado, Wyoming—nearly all the states and territories further west—there was hardly a building that would have been old enough to vote if given the franchise.

From the window of the stagecoach carrying him west from the river steamer *Barlow's Maudie*, Longarm saw elegant homes with broad verandahs and white, slender columns, the sort of house that hadn't been built anywhere in the South since before the recent unpleasantness. There were business blocks built of brick and stone, with walls where generations of ivy clung. A statue in the public square had been in place long enough to be stained with age and crumbling in spots.

This was country that was settled many years back—at least by western standards—and not at all the raw and ready sort of place Longarm was accustomed to seeing.

He looked out at the cramped town lots and the tiny garden patches and the virtual wall of forest surrounding Addington and, if the truth be known, he felt more than a little closed in and overwhelmed. Claustrophobic, he had heard someone call that feeling. Fancy word, that. Penned in and damned uncomfortable played the same tune but on a simpler instrument. Whatever it was called, he didn't much care for it. In country like this a man could find himself in an ambush with a step in any direction and be dead before he could blink his surprise over the fact.

Still, this was the country he was given to work with, and he supposed he would just have to get along as best he might manage. And hopefully not give any would-be ambushers reason to lay for him.

The coach deposited him in front of a three-story-tall hotel building. Three genuine stories at that. He walked down the alley and checked, amazed to discover that the top floor was the real article and not merely a false front.

Since he had no better idea of where to stay he figured this place should be as good as any other and went inside to register.

"And how long will you be staying, sir?" the desk clerk asked.

"I'm not for sure," Longarm admitted. "Could be a couple days. Could be a couple weeks. Damn if I can tell you." He shrugged. "Till the job is done, that's all I know."

"Yes the, um, job. Very good, sir. Shall we agree on the businessman's rate in that event?"

"Meaning?"

"Two dollars a night, sir, and you receive a receipt for purpose of reimbursement. Two twenty-five nightly if you pay by voucher drawn against your employer."

"And if it comes outa my own pocket?" Longarm asked, already suspecting the answer, at least in approximate terms.

The clerk smiled. "A dollar fifty in that event, sir. But, um, you receive certain, shall we say, advantages of comfort if you opt for the business rate."

"Advantages?"

"In the bar, sir. And a, um, discount on the, well, the services of some of the, uh, female . . . entertainers . . . also in the bar."

"I see." Longarm smiled back at the slimy little son of a bitch. "I'll pay the dollar fifty rate, friend. By voucher."

"But . . ."

"The voucher is drawn on the Ewe Ess gov'ment." He reached inside his coat and pulled out both his wallet and a sheaf of the payment vouchers Henry had prepared for him back in Denver. He made sure the cheating SOB on the other side of the counter had plenty of time to look at the badge pinned inside the wallet, then he handed over one of the vouchers. Unsigned. "I'll sign this for you at the end o' my stay, friend. Right after you an' me go over the receipt line by line. That sound good enough t' you, does it?"

"Well, um, yes. Oh my yes, quite acceptable, I'm sure."

Longarm picked up his wallet and put it out of sight. "Reckon we'll get along just fine, friend."

"Yes, I, uh, I'm quite sure we will, mister . . . that is, uh, Marshal . . ." He watched, reading upsidedown, as Longarm signed the guest register. "Long, is it? Marshal Long?"

"That's right." Longarm felt no inclination to invite this unpleasant pipsqueak to call him by his nickname.

"I'll put you in room thirty-two, I think. Third floor rear, and . . ."

"I see on your board that room twenty-six is available. What's it like?"

"Oh, I doubt you would like that one, Marshal. It looks out over the street. Very noisy."

"I'll take twenty-six, I think." The little prick was trying to palm off the least desirable room in the place, Longarm was sure. Top floor, long climb to reach it each night and looking out onto a rooftop and a bunch of pigeon shit, most likely.

"Yes, sir. As you prefer." The fellow handed over the key to 26. And made no offer to help Longarm with his carpetbag and saddle with the heavy Winchester hanging in its scabbard there.

It was a small and petty victory for the little shit, Longarm figured, and one the clerk was entitled to. Since he'd lost in all the other—equally petty—battles.

"G'day," Longarm told him cheerfully and took his things up the stairs in search of room twenty-six.

Chapter 4

Longarm tugged at the gold chain that crossed the front of his vest, dragging a bulbous and somewhat battered but still entirely serviceable Ingersoll key-wind watch from the left-hand vest pocket. Instead of the customary ornate fob the opposite pocket held a small and deadly brass-framed derringer pistol. All in all a satisfyingly useful pair of items were linked by the chain. At the moment the railroad-quality Ingersoll assured him that it was barely past three on a sunny afternoon. Plenty of time to find the local law and announce himself as a federal peace officer operating within the local's jurisdiction, a courtesy that he saw no reason to forgo here.

With a stifled yawn and a mild letdown into relaxation now that the difficulty of the journey from Denver was behind him, Longarm returned the watch to his vest pocket and carefully locked the hotel room door—Number 26 was every bit as pleasant a room as he'd hoped—behind him.

On an impulse driven by mild curiosity he took a detour on his way out, going downstairs by first going upstairs—in search of the room the desk clerk had intended him to take.

He grinned when he found it. Room 32 was large enough to house an alley cat. So long as she didn't have a litter of kittens with her. As a hotel room the facility would have made a right fair custodial closet. And in fact may well have been intended for precisely that use until incipient greed ruled otherwise.

Longarm found himself more amused than annoyed by the clerk's attempt at one-upmanship. Chuckling silently to himself he nipped the end off a cheroot and spat the fleck of tobacco out, then lighted his smoke and headed downstairs again in search of the town marshal.

Chief of police—*not* anything so old-fashioned and primitive as a town marshal here, thank you—J. Michael Bender was on duty at the small jail-cum-police station on the third floor of City Hall, which was one of several municipal buildings facing Addington's town square. City Hall and its lawn occupied half of the block lying immediately east of the square. Behind it a hundred yards or so lay the willow-shaded banks of the Neches River. Massive oak trees and some flowering bushes were dotted here and there on the expanse of grass, presumably a public park, between the three-story city building and the river. It was a handsome scene when viewed from the heights of the police chief's window, and Longarm said so.

"I see," Chief Bender mused. "You've come here at considerable trouble and expense to tell me you like the view from my office, is that it, Deputy?"

Longarm gave the local a tolerant smile. "Chief, what I came here to do is t' look into the murder of an employee of the United States of America. Makin' that murder a federal offense an' putting it under my jurisdiction. I didn't come here t' step on anybody's toes, least of all yours."

"You said your name is Long?"

"I did."

"Then let me tell you something, Deputy Long. You can stand there smug and smiling all day long while you tell me you don't wish to step on my toes. The fact remains, this is my jurisdiction. Not yours. And I resent your presence here. The mere fact of you being here implies that I cannot be trusted to solve a serious crime. It implies . . ."

16

"But I . . ."

"Dammit, sir, you will not interrupt me when I speaking. Do you hear me?"

Longarm grunted, But did not speak. Lordy, no. If he said anything he'd no doubt be accused of interrupting again. Which of course he had done if the man wanted to get real technical about it. Which apparently he did.

One thing about Police Chief Bender, Longarm thought. The man couldn't be accused of being too shy to speak his mind on things. Not damn likely.

"Now. As I was saying, or attempting to say . . . your presence is as good as a slap in my face. An implication that the damnyankee politicians in Washington oppose me. And as I am quite sure both you and they are well aware, sir, we have county elections scheduled in five weeks' time. I take this to be the first salvo of opposition to me and to my fellow party members. Well, sir, I, that is to say we, are not likely to accept this meekly. We will fight you to the last breath and to the last ballot. I can assure you of that much, deputy. Count on it."

Bender looked about as belligerent as a bantam rooster strutting through a hen house. Cocky, full of himself, and damned well on the prod for any challenge that might come into view.

And to give the man his due, it could sure as hell look like what the police chief thought—if somebody didn't know the truth and was so full of politics that he couldn't see simple answers when the mind was so capable of conjuring up complications.

"Chief, I sure as hell would like t' make a peace truce with you right here an' now. I got no use for politics m'self. And I haven't been told t' mix into whatever you folks got going on down here. I didn't know an' frankly don't care that you got your county races coming up. I got no idea how good a police chief you are nor what party you an' your friends belong to an' given the choice would rather not know. Me, I stay outa all that. All I want, Chief, is t' do my job. An' my job is just as simple as simple can be. I wanta find the man

17

that murdered Postmaster Norman Colton. Quick as I got that man, or men, in custody, chief, I'll be outa your jurisdiction an' on my way home. An' that is damn sure the *only* thing I'm s'posed t' do here. I mean that. The only thing.''

Bender gave him a look of blunt skepticism, then cleared his throat and looked away.

''T' help get me outa your hair just as quick as possible, Chief, would you be willing to show me whatever files or records you got relating t' the death of Postmaster Colton?''

What the hell, Longarm thought. If you couldn't expect cheerful cooperation, why not look for whatever sort you could get?

Chapter 5

It was just purely amazing, Longarm thought, how in a town no bigger than Addington, Texas, something as unusual as a murder could take place—well, he assumed it was unusual for there to be a murder here although he supposed that was not necessarily true—and yet nobody in town seemed to know a damn thing about it.

Even more incredible, nobody in the whole town seemed so much as *curious* about it.

Nobody made any guesses as to who it was that shot the postmaster. None of the Addington's citizens seemed inclined even to talk about the murder.

Hell, there was one sawed-off little runt of a fellow who looked Longarm square in the eyes and swore he hadn't been aware that the postmaster was killed.

Incredible!

After a couple hours spent walking through the business district of Addington, Longarm hadn't managed to find a solitary soul who was willing to talk to him about the murder of a fellow citizen. A man as prominent as the postmaster, at that.

Why, a coincidence like that was damn near enough to make Longarm think folks here didn't want an outsider messing about in their business.

Or something.

Still, he had an ace in the hole, a tried-and-true, never-fail method for extracting information—or at the very least some good ol' rumors—when all else failed.

He headed for the nearest barbershop and asked for a shave and a trim. He hadn't yet met the barber who wasn't anxious to spill everything he knew to every customer whose butt hit his chair.

"Trim those nose hairs for you, mister?" the barber offered.

"Yes, thanks." Longarm closed his eyes and let the barber take control, the sound of clattering scissors a pleasant, rather soothing undertone.

"I don't believe you've been in before today, have you?"

"No, sir. New in town."

"Uh huh." The barber's shears clicked and rattled as the man began trimming the back of Longarm's neck. "Figure to stay a while?"

"Likely not. I have to take care of a little business here, then I'll have to move along."

"Uh-huh." The barber switched to a different set of clippers, the blade chill on Longarm's skin, and snipped away.

"Somebody on the stagecoach said you had some excitement here a while back," Longarm ventured.

"Is that so? He must have meant the county fair. You missed that by a couple weeks. Pity too. There was a tent show where if you paid an extra dime you could go into the little tent out back of the big one. They had them some dancing girls there whee-oow, mister, you should of seen them. Took off every stitch, I'm telling you. Every stitch. One of them women, mister, had her pussy hair shaved into the shape of a heart. Now I been a barber going on thirty years and I never seen a thing like that before, let me tell you. And her titties, they were hanging right out, bouncing and jiggling and flopping all over. Yes sir, that was some excitement, all right." The clippers nipped and rattled as the barber deftly, rapidly squeezed them.

"That, uh, isn't what this fellow on the coach meant, I

20

think. He said something about there being a murder here? Now that surprised me, see. A nice-looking town like this, you don't think in terms of murder and shootings and the like.''

"You don't?" the barber asked.

"Well I wouldn't think so.''

"Really? Now friend, I would've thought that a United States deputy marshal would pretty nigh always be thinking in terms of murders and shootings and things like that there,'' the barber offered.

Longarm opened his eyes. The barber was grinning.

"You got to understand that this is a small town. Word goes around fast anyway. And, Marshal, you've been stomping up and down our streets for the better part of two hours now. I would have noticed you even if folks hadn't been talking about there being a federal man snooping around.''

"That's what I like,'' Longarm declared. "An honest man.''

The barber chuckled and went back to cutting hair. "I think you will find, Marshal, that most folks hereabouts are honest. A mite shy with strangers sometimes, but honest.''

"That's real nice to know, friend.''

"Lay your head on back now. I'm ready to lather and shave you.'' He picked up the strop that dangled from a hook attached to the back of the barber chair and began freshening the edge of one of his razors.

"You have a nice touch,'' Longarm said a few moments later as the thin sliver of tempered steel moved featherlight across his flesh.

"Thank you. Like I said, I been at this near thirty years now.''

"You wouldn't happen to know . . .''

"About those girls in the tent show? Sure. Be glad to tell you everything I can about them, marshal. What is it you'd like to know?''

Apparently even this otherwise friendly man was not going to tell him anything about the death of Norman Colton. Dammit. Longarm shrugged and accepted the inevitable, letting the barber finish without further distraction.

Chapter 6

The post office was closed by the time Longarm got there, locked up for the night and with no sign of the acting postmaster who was replacing the murdered man. Longarm gave it up for the time being and walked back to his hotel.

Supper was a dull affair, the beef boiled, stringy, and tough and the mashed potatoes gray and unappealing. The hotel cook somehow even managed to make apple pie taste like lightly sweetened library paste, an accomplishment of some note if not of any great worth. And to top it all off the cigars they handed out after dinner were so dry and dusty, the wrapper cracked when he tried to cut the twist off the tip. With a grimace of distaste he tossed the miserable thing onto his soiled plate—let them wipe the gravy off if they wanted to salvage it to present to some other poor SOB tomorrow—and pulled out one of his own slim cheroots.

Not willing to trust the bar in a place where the food was so bad, he wandered outside in search of a way to spend some time until he might become sleepy.

A logical choice presented itself two blocks south in the form of a lively, friendly seeming little saloon that offered exactly what Longarm craved at the moment: no tin-pan piano noise, no painted women, no stage show or so-called entertainment whatsoever—just whiskey, beer, and a few tables where a man might choose to talk or deal a hand of cards. In short, it was just right.

"Friend, I almost hate t' ask you this lest I destroy the pleasure of the moment . . . but would you happen t' have a bottle of Maryland-distilled rye whiskey?"

The bartender grinned. "Would Tomlin Brothers do?"

"Who'd have thought it?" Longarm asked. "A man that actually knows good booze."

"The best of the best, that's what the Tomlin boys bottle." He laughed. "I know 'cause I was raised from a pup on the shores of the old Patuxent, and my best boyhood friend was a grandson of one of the original Tomlins who founded the business. D'you know the label?"

"Well enough to revere the brothers Tomlin and all their kith and kin."

"In that case, neighbor, the first one is on me." He winked and added, "And I believe I shall have a free one with you."

"Done and done," Longarm declared. He accepted the tall shot of smoky whiskey with pleasure and savored the warmth of it on his tongue and the cozy glow that spread through his belly afterward. "Ah now, that's even better than I remembered."

"Refill?"

"Yes, and one for you as well. My treat this time."

The barman poured two full measures, then left the bottle where Longarm could reach it while he hurried away down the bar to tend to the needs of his other patrons.

This, Longarm thought, was a cut above the cold, inhospitable hotel and then some.

The second drink went down slower and even smoother than the first, then he gave himself a third and turned to survey the room.

After a moment his eyes widened slightly with pleased surprise and, drink in hand, he ambled toward the back corner where a foursome of gents in business suits were dealing draw poker.

As he came closer to the table a smile tugged at the corners

23

of his mouth, and his hand started forward in the offer of a shake.

A slightly built, suntanned fellow in tweed with a dusty bowler perched on the back of his dark, tousled hair jumped up to greet him with a mildly overloud, "Hello there, stranger, are you looking to join our game, sit right in and welcome, my name is Colton, sir, Lester Colton of Liberty County, and your name would be . . . ?" He got it all out in one long rush, without pausing for breath.

Longarm stopped still for half a heartbeat, then gravely nodded and took the offered handshake.

"Colton, you said?"

"I did, sir, Lester Colton from down in Liberty County."

"My name is Long, Mr. Colton. Custis Long, but you can call me Longarm, which all my friends do, old or new."

"Then I hope to call you Longarm, sir."

"Please do that, Mr. Colton," Longarm said, his face impassive but his eyes sparkling with contained amusement as he addressed himself to his old friend—and, when last Longarm looked, Texas Ranger—Amos Vent.

Chapter 7

Longarm belched, swaying sideways and damn near falling off his chair. A couple of the other players frowned at the unseemly display. The gent who was the evening's big winner, a banker named Tony, seemed quite comfortable, however, with the idea of having a drunk participate in the play. And if this fellow named Long hadn't yet become reckless enough to begin losing heavily, well, surely another few slugs out of that bottle of rye whiskey and the tap would open and winnings in large measure commence pouring onto the table.

"I c'n open," Longarm said, blinking.

"Pay attention, man. Louis already opened. You can stay for a dime or fold, Long. Which?"

Longarm blinked again and unsteadily pushed a dime in the general direction of the pot. To Longarm's immediate left, the man who was calling himself Lester Colton dropped his cards face down onto the table and shook his head. The banker raised and when it came around to him again Longarm once more had to be told what to put up if he wanted to stay in the game. He blinked and wobbled and after some hemming and hawing raised the bet a dollar. Tony began to smile.

"Cards, gentlemen?"

Longarm reached to discard first this card, then that one,

finally deciding to take two out of the middle and toss them onto the pile of rejects.

After that the betting was heavy indeed, with Tony, Louis, a merchant named Greg and another named Jason vying to see which one of them would be allowed the privilege of taking Longarm's money.

"Bets, gentlemen? Louis?"

"Fifty cents."

"Long?"

"I'll bet . . . I'll bet . . . I'll bet . . . what've I got here? Five? Bet fi' dollars." He belched. " 'Scuse me." He made a noise that was probably supposed to be a laugh but instead came out sounding more like a giggle. He pushed a pile of small change totaling five and a half dollars onto the by-now rather large pot.

"Five fifty to you, Tony."

"Call."

"Call."

"Me too."

The others showed their hands, the results ranging from a pair of kings to a high of three nines.

Longarm leaned forward, as if trying to concentrate . . . and falling short of what was needed.

"Let us look at your hand, Marshal," Amos Vent, otherwise known as Lester Colton, prompted.

"What? Oh. Yeah. Han'. Right." He dropped his cards onto the table, spread into a fan shape. He held a full house, aces over treys.

"Shit," the distinguished banker grumbled.

"Do I win?" Longarm asked of no one in particular.

"Yes, you win. Let me help you with that money. And I tell you what else, if you don't mind a suggestion."

"Go 'head. Su'gest."

"I think you've had about enough fun for one night, Deputy. Let me help you back to your room. You're at the hotel, are you?"

"I th . . . thi . . . thing so. Yeah. Hotel. Damn ri', at the ol' hotel."

"All right then." Colton nodded to his companions at the table. "If you will please excuse us, gentlemen? I believe the good marshal here is done for the night."

There was no disagreement with the plan, and Colton helped Longarm shove winnings into his coat pockets, then pretty much picked the much larger man up and slung one sagging arm over his own thin shoulders to help Longarm on his way.

With Longarm weaving and staggering and loudly trying to sing a poorly remembered sea chanty, Colton managed to get out of the saloon and down the street to the hotel where a disgusted desk clerk handed over Longarm's key and gave directions to the appropriate room.

It seemed all Colton could do to get Longarm up the staircase without losing him in an end-over-end tumble back down into the lobby, but by dint of much pulling and tugging he got the job done.

He found the correct room, unlocked it and unceremoniously dumped Longarm onto the bed, then turned and shut and bolted the door.

At which point Amos Vent and Custis Long both went into great roaring gasps of laughter.

"My god, Longarm, didn't you think you were overdoing it toward the end there? I swear I thought I was gonna bust a gut from trying to not laugh out loud and spoil it for you."

"They bought it, didn't they?"

"Yes, but it seems an awful lot of trouble just to win a couple dollars."

Longarm grinned. "Twenty-some bucks to the good. Hell, Amos, I've worked a lot of full months for less'n that. An' I expect you have too."

"That I have," the smallish Ranger agreed.

"An' anyway, it wasn't winning a pot that I had in mind. I figured we needed some excuse t' get you up here t' where we could talk in private an' afterward be seen acting friendly even though we ain't supposed t' know each other. Well, I'd say it's worked out all right.''

''I kinda thought that was what you wanted.''

Longarm chuckled and, quite sober now that no one else was watching, pulled out cheroots for himself and for his old friend. ''Now sit down an' start talking, Amos, an' don't even think about quitting until you've filled me in on why you're playacting like a dead man's long-lost kin. Or whatever the hell it is you're supposed t' be here.''

Vent accepted the smoke and helped himself to a seat in the room's one comfortable chair, crossing his legs and leaning back to enjoy the flavor of the smoke for a moment. Then, a much more serious expression replacing the playfulness in his eyes, he leaned forward and set in to giving Longarm the requested explanations.

Chapter 8

Politics. Damn, Longarm hated politics. It only served to get in the way of any honest effort to enforce laws.

But politics was something a lawman damn sure had to deal with. And too often.

This right here was a case in point.

Texas state politics and U.S. government-level politics and local politics were all mixed up together here.

Amos Vent explained that. More or less. The truth seemed to be that Amos himself wasn't sure about all of it, at least not to the extent of knowing where the bodies were buried or even who it was in town here that could point to the burial spots.

Amos was here pretending to be the dead man's cousin—with an interest in the handling of the late postmaster's estate—because there were state politicians in Austin who were ordering the Texas attorney general, and through him the Texas Rangers, to lay off Addington so the local power brokers wouldn't be offended. It had something to do with the state people needing the support of some of the powerful locals to get something voted through the state legislature. And at the same time there was another faction that wanted to be able to accomplish this without riling certain folks at the federal level in Washington. And then there was supposed to be some ebb and flow of power here at the local level, but neither Longarm nor Amos knew what the hell that was supposed to be about.

It was a mess, that's what it was, Longarm figured. As political interference always was.

But then all Longarm wanted was to find out who the hell killed Norman Colton. And then go home.

"What I can't understand," Longarm muttered at length, "is what the hell I'm doin' here."

Amos gave him a sheepish look.

"You know something 'bout that, Amos?"

"I, uh, guess I do at that."

"Well?"

"My boss sent me here undercover, you know, so we could be sure the job was getting done and yet not let those people in Austin know that we were ignoring their message to lay off. You can understand that, I'm sure."

"To a point, yeah. Me, I'd go ahead an' rub their noses in it. But then it ain't my decision t' make."

"I might prefer to do that myself, but it wasn't my decision either. Anyway, back to the point of all this, when my boss was telling me how he wanted it handled he was worried about what might happen when a U.S. deputy marshal came along to put that oar in the water. Which we naturally knew was going to happen sooner or later no matter how much pressure the boys from Austin tried to apply in Washington. I mean, you fellas keep yourselves mostly free of politics. More than we can manage, though we sure do try."

Longarm nodded and puffed on his cheroot, content to wait for Amos to continue at his own pace.

"I got to tell you, asking for you to come in on this thing, you in particular that is, was my idea. Like I said, we knew there would have to be someone involved from the federal level. There didn't seem any way around that. And I figured as good as you and I get along, well, if it was you they assigned down here we could talk it out. Like we're doing now. And I knew we could count on you to not blow any whistles

30

on us. I mean, everyone in town here knows you're carrying a badge and have legal jurisdiction. They might not like it, but they understand it. And it's no secret. Me they shouldn't know about. And don't have to. I figure we can work together on this thing, Longarm, and when the time comes you can be the one to make any arrests or ask for warrants or whatever else might be involved. That way no one will ever have to know there was a Ranger here, and my boss won't be in jeopardy of losing his job to the whims of a bunch of assholes with deep pockets and more interest in votes than in justice."

"Just figured you could use me any ol' way you wanted, did you?" Longarm asked.

Amos grinned. "Something like that, yeah."

"Well, I expect you were right. Reckon I'll go along with your plan." Longarm grinned back at his old friend. "But I got t' tell you, my boss got kinda peeved at having one o' his people requested an' nobody knowing why or by who. Bothered him some, it did."

"Nothing serious, I hope."

"He'll get over it."

"I know he used to be a Ranger himself and knows a lot of the people still in government in Austin. It might be a good idea if you don't explain it to him, not all of it, even after it's over, Longarm. You never know if somebody else can keep his mouth shut, and your Marshal Vail still has a lot of friends in Texas."

"It's true that he does," Longarm agreed. But very carefully did not make any promises to Amos Vent. Promises that Longarm would have had no intention of keeping. After all, Billy Vail was entitled to full knowledge of what his own officers did—never mind what the Texas Rangers might want him to know. Or not.

But there was no sense in making Amos nervous about that. Better to just let the Ranger think Longarm was agreeable. But, hell, if Longarm couldn't trust Billy Vail then he'd best hand in his badge and go look for another line of work. Billy was as good a man as Custis Long had ever known, and Long-

31

arm would trust Billy as completely as he would trust himself.

"You'll work with me then, Longarm? On the quiet?"

"I will that, Amos. Excuse me, I mean t' say that I will work with you, on the quiet, plain ol' ordinary citizen Lester Colton."

Amos chuckled and asked, "Now that that's out of the way, d'you happen to have a bottle of that good rye whiskey in your bag like you usually do?"

"It's wrapped inside my clean shirts. Dig it out an' help yourself if you like."

Amos stood and began searching in Longarm's carpetbag for the hidden treasure.

Chapter 9

"You're Long?"

Longarm looked up from his stack of sorghum-soaked hot-cakes. "You must be Short."

He regretted it even before the last sounds passed out of his stupid, unthinking mouth. Because the truth is that short men damn seldom want the fact pointed out to them. And this sawed-off runt was shorter than most. Hell, he probably couldn't hit the five-foot-four mark unless he was wearing boots. Short, built like a pint-sized bull and with a brushy flare of whisker so wide and full it looked like he was trying to compensate for his other shortcomings all in one lump of flaming red hair.

"Smartass son of a bitch, aren't you," the man accused.

"I got to give credit where it's due, neighbor. You got balls to say that to my face."

"There are those that call me Brass. Does that tell you anything?"

"It does." The name fit remarkably well in several different ways, starting with the little man's belligerent manner and extending through the bright, brassy color of his hair and right on down to the brass frame of the big revolver that rode high at his waist. The gun was something of an anachronism in this modern day and age, an old-fashioned cap-and-ball Remington

33

that had been converted to cartridge use some time after it left the factory. Longarm hadn't seen anything like it in a good many years. Brass. Yeah, there was a lot about this little guy that made the name fit. "And in answer to your question, yes, I'm U.S. Deputy Marshal Long. An' you are . . . ?"

"George Braxton, sergeant, Company F of the Texas Rangers stationed over at Nacogdoches."

"Is that so?" Longarm's puzzlement did not have to be feigned. He and Amos Vent—Texas Ranger Amos Vent, that is—had sat up sharing Longarm's supply of rye whiskey until some time past two this morning. And never once had Amos mentioned there being any other Rangers assigned to this political stewpot in Addington, Texas. Which quite assuredly meant that Amos hadn't been aware of Brass George Braxton's presence. Could be that the captain of this F Company of Rangers was acting apart from the interests of the bossman back in Austin. Or then again it could be for a perfectly innocent reason, like for instance Amos's boss in Austin wasn't letting any of his subordinates in on the undercover assignment and so the F Company commander was simply trying to do his job while being unaware of the hidden interests down in Austin. All in all kinda interesting, Longarm thought. And— thank goodness—none of his nevermind. All he had to worry about was one dead postmaster and the man who killed him. Amos and his fellow Rangers, here or in Austin or Nacogdoches or wherever the hell else, could take care of the rest of it.

"Sit down, Sergeant. Join me for breakfast." Longarm kicked a chair back from the table and nodded to it.

"I've had my breakfast," Braxton said crossly. "What I want with you, Long, is a word."

"Fine. Set. Have some coffee. Say whatever's on your mind," Longarm invited.

"You don't get it, do you?"

"That you ain't feeling friendly? Sergeant, the gravel in your craw is rattling loud an' clear. Now I don't know what's put it there an' I don't much care. I got no cause to have a mad on with you nor with the Rangers nor with anybody else around here. I'm just tryin' to mind my own business an' do a job. But if you know something that I don't, well, feel free t' spit it out. Right out in the open. I'll listen to whatever you want t' tell me.''

"All right. I'll tell you the plain truth, Long. You are not wanted here. You are not needed here. You would be well advised to leave here. Is that clear enough?''

"It is, sergeant, and I thank you for your honesty.''

Earlier Braxton had looked like he was ready for a fight. Now he only looked confused. "Is that it? You aren't going to quarrel with me?''

"Quarrel, Sergeant? Hell no. Whyever should I go an' do that. I asked you t' say what was on your mind an' you said it. I got no beef with you over that.''

"And you'll leave now?''

"Pay attention, Sergeant. I thanked you for your honesty. I didn't say nothing about acting on what you had t' say.''

"You won't leave,'' Braxton said sourly.

"I will leave,'' Longarm told him, adding to the sawed-off Ranger sergeant's obvious confusion. "Like I told the police chief yesterday, sergeant, I only come here t' do one thing. That's to investigate the murder of an employee o' the United States government. Which as you, me an' him all know is within my jurisdiction. I figure t' do that, Sergeant, an' then I will quick as can be get the hell outa this town an' go report back to my boss.''

"But you are staying here for now.''

"If you want me out in a hurry, Sergeant, tell the police chief to let me look through his files on the Colton killing. It could save us all some time an' get me outa your hair the soonest possible.''

"You aren't needed here, Long.''

"Then help me get done in a hurry, Sergeant.''

"My commander doesn't want you here. The local law doesn't want you here. And the leaders of this community don't want you here.''

35

"You want the addresses so you can write t' my boss in Denver an' to the Attorney General o' these United States? Give me a pencil an' I'll mark them down for you."

"We already know . . ."

"Yeah, o' course you do. But Sergeant, you'll stay here an' follow your captain's orders till he hollers whoa. Me, I'll do the same till I hear otherwise from Marshal Billy Vail. D'you hear what I'm telling you?"

"I hear."

"Fine. An' now that we've growled at one another all we need to," Longarm grinned, "whyn't you set down an' have some hotcakes with me? They're mighty good but gettin' cold, an' if I have t' be polite much longer they ain't gonna be fit to eat when I get around to them. So set down an' let the U.S. gummint buy you a breakfast. Which isn't an offer you're gonna get just every day o' the week, you know."

After a moment's hesitation Sergeant Braxton relented and took the seat Longarm was offering.

Chapter 10

"Sergeant? The chief would like to see you, sir." The kid who had stopped at the table was young, fresh faced and barely old enough to begin shaving. He looked like a high school boy despite his attire, which consisted of wrinkled trousers, heavy brogans and a dark blue coat with its brass buttons fastened clear to the throat. He also wore a remarkably stupid-looking billed cap with gaudy brass sunburst device pinned above the polished leather bill. He wore, in short, the uninspired uniform of a local police officer.

"And what is it that he needs, Willy?" Braxton asked in return.

The young copper quite obviously had been given no instructions regarding Longarm—if indeed he had any inkling who this other man at the table was—or he probably would not have responded so freely. "There's been another murder, sergeant. Just like the other ones."

Other ones? Longarm's interest was definitely aroused once he heard that most unexpected term. What damned other "ones"—plural, as in more than one other, eh?

"Right away," Braxton agreed, and the kid cop spun on his heels and trotted quickly away, presumably to alert Police Chief Bender that help was on its way in the form of the ever vigilant Texas Rangers.

"Reckon I'll follow along if you don't mind," Longarm drawled as he reached into a pocket for change to leave on the table in payment of his meal and Braxton's.

"I don't think . . ."

"Just so you can ask the chief t' let me see those records about Colton. Like you promised. Right?"

Braxton frowned. But there really was little he could say in response except that of course the request was a reasonable one. After all, the federal man was making no claims about jurisdiction here; he was merely asking for information about his own case. And never mind that it was plain the Ranger sergeant would have much preferred for Long to stay right where he was and eat another stack of hotcakes or something.

The two peace officers stood, and Longarm followed Brass Braxton out onto the street while off in a far corner the man who called himself Lester Colton was finishing a breakfast of his own.

"It was Pete Nare, George. Shot down sometime during the night. Nobody seems to have heard the shot fired so we don't know when it happened. Pete lived in an apartment above the store, you know. Far as I can learn, he closed at his usual time last night. Don't know if he went out after that or not. I'll ask around, of course, to see if he got into any arguments. But you know Pete. He wasn't the kind to look for trouble. Never has been. He was wearing his nightshirt and carpet slippers. Went downstairs, I suppose to answer a knock at the door. What he got was a bullet smack between the eyes. Just like . . ." Glancing at Longarm, who was pretending no interest in the conversation but was certainly hanging close enough to hear every word, Chief Bender suppressed whatever if was he might have been about to say. He cleared his throat and shifted directions. "Small-caliber bullet, it was. Fired at real close range. There are powder burns around the wound. My guess would be the gun was fired point blank, from a foot away or less."

"So someone came in the middle of the night and knocked

38

on the door, then shot Pete down in cold blood when he opened up.''

"That's what it looks like. Pete dropped right on the spot. Didn't even bleed much. He was lying there beside the door when old Jimmy Donovan came in this morning. Jimmy sweeps up . . . that is, he used to . . . for Pete before Pete opened for business each morning. Pete let Jimmy use his shed to sleep in and sometimes gave Jimmy a little money too.''

"And Donovan didn't hear anything during the night, Mike? Are you sure?''

"Dammit, George, you know Donovan. He hasn't spent a sober evening . . . not outside a jail cell, he hasn't . . . in fifteen, twenty years. Not if he could help it. Jimmy was passed out cold last night just like always. He wouldn't have heard it if somebody decided to hold artillery firing drills on the town square last night.''

"No, I suppose not. And Pete? Do you think he knew his killer? Or did he just respond to the knock thinking there was a customer who needed something in the middle of the night?''

"No way to tell that, is there?'' Chief Bender asked rhetorically. After yet another glance toward Longarm.

Braxton saw the direction the chief's look was going and quickly responded, "No, of course not. No way to tell that at all.''

Longarm was commencing to find their circumspection damn near amusing. "About those records, sergeant?''

"Oh, yeah. Mike, I told the deputy here that I'd ask you to help him out with something. In the interest of a speedy investigation. If, um, you know what I mean.''

Five minutes later, Longarm and the Addington police department's file on the murder of Norman Colton were comfortably settled at a desk in the police chief's own private office.

While, unfortunately, the murder of shopkeeper Pete Nare was discussed outside of Longarm's hearing.

Other murders, Longarm kept thinking. Plural. Meaning

there now had been at least three recent killings in Addington. Or possibly even more.

Yet no one, dammit, wanted to talk to him.

With luck, though, the file on Norman Colton might help.

Chapter 11

Longarm tried to be fair about it. Shit, he hated paperwork himself and avoided that drudgery whenever possible. It could be that Chief Bender felt the same. Or it was also possible that there was some other reason why the case file on the murder of the town's postmaster was so skimpy.

Whatever the reason, though, the information provided by Bender was not likely to result in a shouted "aha." Longarm learned damned little from it beyond the bare-bones facts. Postmaster Colton had been alone in the post office after closing for the day. Party or parties unknown apparently knocked at the back door. When Colton opened the door he was shot in the forehead at very close range. The bullet recovered from his brain was a pipsqueak .32-caliber slug. No one remembered hearing a gunshot at the time, but then that afternoon there were a good many muted explosions in the streets and alleys of the town as small boys set off firecrackers. The relatively soft report of a .32-caliber revolver would have been lost in the rest of the noise. Colton's body was discovered that evening when he failed to show up at his customary Wednesday-night card game, and some of his friends went looking so as to remind him that it was time to start playing.

For the third time Longarm read the file through, end to end, without learning anything new, then closed the file and placed it carefully on the center of the chief's desk top before stepping out to thank the chief and the Ranger sergeant for all their help and cooperation. Hoping, of course, that they would both choke on the sentiment.

He was disappointed, though. The outer office was empty, everyone presumably having traipsed off to look into this latest of Addington's murders.

Longarm hesitated for half a moment, then with a grunt and a shrug went back into the chief's office.

Another half a moment and he grunted again. Damn police chief wasn't a very trusting soul. His file cabinet and desk were both locked, and with good locks at that. Longarm could open them. But not without leaving visible traces of the burglary. Dammit.

And since he wasn't real sure Chief Bender would accept a claim that he was only breaking into the files in order to return the Colton folder to its proper place, Longarm decided to leave things as he found them.

But it was a pity to waste the opportunity.

Accepting fate as he found it, Longarm lighted a cheroot and ambled out of the police station and headed back in the direction of his hotel.

Chapter 12

"Buy me a drink, cowboy?"

The woman asking the question—or making the offer, which was somewhat more accurate—was one damned fine-looking filly. Twenty or thirty years ago.

By now she was more than a little shopworn and bedraggled.

She had copper-colored hair that looked like it was beginning to tarnish from overexposure to the elements, streaks of dirt caked in the folds of flesh under her chin, and tits that might once have been magnificent but which now were drooping toward her kneecaps . . . and damn near completing the journey.

"I'm not a cowboy, lady."

She laughed, the sound of it hearty and indeed quite genuine as she responded, "And I'm no lady, cowboy."

Longarm chuckled. "Thanks for the invite, ma'am, but it's a mite early in the day for that. I only came in looking for a bite o' lunch."

"All right. No drink. Buy me some lunch instead."

"Persistent, ain't you?"

She hooted loudly, pretending he'd said something outrageously funny, and gripped his arm as she leaned forward and licked his earlobe. While she was in the neighborhood she whispered, very softly, "I want to talk to you, Marshal. In private."

"Whyn't you and me have that drink in my room, lady," he suggested. Loudly enough that anyone who wanted to overhear was welcome, and able, to do so.

"A lovely idea, cowboy," she said, gathering up her skirts in one hand and her handbag in the other.

Chapter 13

He hadn't any more than gotten the door closed than the damn woman was on him like a barn cat after a field mouse. She was trying her level best to suck his tongue clean out of his mouth. Or maybe she was kissing him. He wasn't exactly sure which she had in mind.

She smelled of cheap perfume and cheaper whiskey, and he was fairly certain that she'd had sardines for breakfast.

Being kissed by this no longer handsome female was not one of the finer pleasures of life.

After a bit of a struggle—fortunately he was bigger, stronger, and possibly meaner than she was, and managed to extract his tongue from her mouth without having to actually punch her—he backed warily away and pointed her at the lone chair in the hotel room. NOT, thank you, at the bed.

"You, uh, said you wanted t' talk?" he suggested.

She smiled at him. "Yes, Marshal. That too."

"Too?"

"After you screw me."

"But . . ."

"I love to screw, Marshal." She batted her eyelashes at him, a quite perfectly ludicrous come-on that she herself laughed at, delighted with the silliness of her own gesture. "Am I shocking you?"

45

"It takes a lot t' shock me, ma'am." He grinned. "But you're coming pretty nigh to it."

She laughed appreciatively and said, "Allow me to introduce myself. I am Jane Webster Sproul of the Carolina Websters and widow of the late Judge Walker Martin Sproul. Which probably means absolutely nothing to you but which is quite a mouthful for anyone who grew up around these parts." She laughed again. And there was something in the open, honest ring of her voice when she laughed that warned Longarm that if she didn't quit it pretty damn soon he might actually commence to like this odd woman. "And you, I believe, are named Long, are you not?"

"I am, ma'am. Custis Long. Longarm t' my friends."

"Then I hope I shall be permitted to so address you."

On an impulse, bowing low and saying, "Permission granted, ma'am."

She clapped her hands. And leaped off the chair to bound across the room—well, it was only a couple steps but she managed to convey an impression of great bounding . . . and in fact her massive tits flopped so wildly that she might as well have been bounding over a series of fences to reach him—and envelop him in a hug. And in a repeat of her wet, loose kiss as well.

"Now I know why everybody else in this town is s' damn unfriendly," he said once he had the use of his mouth back.

"And what reason would that be, dear friend Longarm?"

"It's because you got the friendliness market cornered, Janie. There's none left over for them others t' use."

She threw her head back and roared. Then turned and, just as casual as if it was the most normal and natural thing possible, began removing articles of clothing and dropping them onto the chair.

Longarm was beginning to get the idea that this interview was not going according to plan. Not to his plan anyhow.

"If you hear talk about me, friend Longarm, and I certainly hope you will, there are several things you should keep in mind. One is that I do what I damn please. I never let other people's opinions stand in the way of a good time. Or anything else, for that matter. Another thing is that there is more than enough reason for most people around here to be jealous of me. You see, I am without question the richest woman within a hundred-mile radius. Or possibly further.'' By now she was down to her lacy smallclothes but showed no signs of slowing down, continuing to shed cloth like a molting hen in a wind storm.

"Another thing to bear in mind, my friend, is that most of what you hear will quite probably be true. If you hear something outrageous, that is. I love to tweak these fools' noses, and for some reason plain, simple, pleasant sex is a good way to do that. Can you imagine? Why would anyone care what anyone else does in bed? Or with whom?'' She tossed the last wisps of lace onto the chair and turned, huge and flabby and about as appealing to look at as a three-days-dead trout, to display herself in all her glory.

"You see, my dear new friend, this has always amazed me but never discouraged me. The simple truth is that I like sex. More, I love sex. I just plain adore the feel of a stiff poker in my snatch. I love the sight, the texture, the taste of something nice and hard. And I love to feel them inside me. Anywhere inside me. . . . I love it all. If you can think of a way to get one into a nostril or an ear canal I'm game to try the position. You know?'' She giggled and flopped onto the bed, legs asprawl and her furry mound prominent.

"I've loved it ever since Randy . . . isn't that a perfectly delightful name for a girl's first beau? . . . ever since Randy Travers grabbed my tit . . . at the time it was hardly big enough to be grabbed, actually . . . and put a hand under my skirt to feel me up. That was at my thirteenth-birthday party. We were playing hide-and-seek, and Randy and I were both hiding in the hay loft.'' She laughed again. "It took them a hell of a time to find us, let me tell you. Long enough for me to get off four, five times right in a row there. The first couple times from Randy fingering me and the rest when he put his cock in me. He didn't want to. Can you imagine? He thought he

47

was scaring me when he shoved his finger in me. Ha! He's the one who ended up scared. I liked it so much I wouldn't let him go until he satisfied me. But he got over being scared. Randy and I went at it nearly every day the summer after my birthday that year. Then Randy enlisted and went off to the war.'' Her expression changed, becoming wistful and slightly sad. ''He never came back, of course. He was fifteen when he left. I never heard how old he made it to before he got himself killed. Clumsy little guy. He wasn't much, poor Randy. But in his own way he loved me.''

She sighed. ''He was my first, though of course no one ever knew. Not until years later.'' Her mood brightened. ''He certainly was not the last, though. I tell you truly, I loved it and I still do. But one thing you have to know. I have never, ever, not in my whole life taken anything in exchange for screwing. Not money, not secrets, not favors, not anything like that. I spread my legs for the pleasure of it, dear friend Longarm. Not for any other reason. And don't you let anybody, I mean not any living soul, try and tell you otherwise. Promise me that, will you? Please?''

''Janie, I believe you. Indeed I do.''

Her smile was sweet and soft. ''Thank you, dear friend Longarm.'' She opened her arms wide. And her legs as well. ''Now come over her, cowboy, and give me some fun.''

''I thought you wanted . . .''

''To talk? Of course. But later, okay? First we screw, then we talk afterward. Now come here, sweetie, before I get so wet I'll drench your bed and you won't be able to sleep dry the whole time you're here.''

Now just what the *hell* was a man supposed to do when faced with a flabby, homely, naked female that he really did not want to screw? He didn't want to insult her, dammit. But he didn't want to crawl on top of her either. Janie Sproul reminded him of one of those female spiders that takes a mate and then kills the used-up little sonuvabitch by sucking all the juices out of its body afterward.

Looking at Janie lying there with one saucer-sized nipple

tucked into each armpit . . . well . . . it wasn't a sight to promote a hard-on, that was for sure.

Yet the truth was that he kinda liked her. For her honesty if nothing else.

And she was the only human person in Addington—the only one other than Amos Vent, that is, and Amos didn't count because he didn't know a thing more than Longarm did about the true situation here—who was willing to talk to him.

So what the hell were his choices about this?

Climb onboard and see what—or who—came next? Or reject the offer and probably make an enemy of the only damn friend he'd found here?

There were times, Longarm reflected, when duty asked an awful lot of a man.

"Sweetheart?" Janie prompted, reaching down to finger herself and pull her snatch wide open, resulting in the display of something that looked remarkably similar to a leather valise laid ready to receive ten or twelve pounds of important documents.

Longarm managed a weak smile. He swallowed. Hard. And wondered if passing out in a dead faint would help.

Chapter 14

Janie Sproul was, well, to be honest about it, Longarm concluded, the woman just wasn't a very good piece of ass.

She was flabby. Which wasn't so bad really except that she was flabby all over. *In*side as well as out. She'd been used so long and so often—he had no opinion as to how well—that her pussy was loose, sloppy, and stretched so far that he could scarcely feel any contact with her.

Which was distracting as all billy hell.

He grunted and wallowed, wriggled this way and then that, poked and prodded . . . nothing he did seemed to result in much in the way of feeling.

And the truth is that it takes more than a good idea for a man to get his rocks off. He has to feel . . . well . . . something, anyway. A little heat, a modicum of feeling . . . some damn thing has to be there if it is going to be any good for him.

As for Janie, shit, she seemed to be having the screw of a lifetime, at least judging by the way she moaned and quivered and carried on.

True to her word, the damn woman yelped and hollered and got herself off half a dozen times. If not by actual count, then not far from it. Seemed like every thirty seconds or so she would shudder and tremble and growl, ''I'm coming, oh, oh, I'm coming, cowboy.''

And he would poke around some more in that great, damp emptiness that was her, and sure enough, a couple seconds later she'd grab on with arms, legs, teeth, and eyeballs while she went through another set of spasms.

After a while Longarm commenced to get somewhat jealous. Why the hell should she have all the fun?

"Pull your legs together."

"What, honey?"

"Your legs," he repeated. "Put them together." He lifted himself off the mattress a bit so she could bring her legs under his thighs, and when she did that he was lying atop her somewhat more than ample body, his legs outside hers so he was the one doing the straddling except that his cock, fortunately more than long enough to permit the method, was still inside her. That squeezed her lips together and made it if not actually tight then at least close enough that he could tell he was inside something. Before it had felt kind of like dipping his wick into a pot of lukewarm machine oil. Not exactly thrilling.

"Oh, I do like this," she said once she felt what he'd done. "Tight."

"Uh-huh," he lied. It was still a helluva long way from tight. But it was damn sure better.

"Oh. Honey. I'm coming."

Shit, he hadn't hardly moved again. But it was enough for Janie. She bellowed and gave him a bear hug and like to shook herself to pieces with the power of this latest in her long line of climaxes.

"Honey, you're so good I can't hardly stand it." Which he assumed was not a complaint. "Harder, honey, harder. Yes, yes, I'm coming, oh jeez I'm coming again."

And damned if she didn't.

It occurred to him that generally speaking when a woman has more than one orgasm it makes a fellow feel kind of pleased with himself. In this particular case, though, Longarm didn't feel entitled to much in the way of credit. With ol' Janie he figured it likely that a decent-looking feather duster would be enough to get her off.

Still and all . . .

"Harder, honey, faster, yes, yes, yes . . ."

Janie was humping and bucking, and now there was a mite of feeling to go with all the sweat and strain and pretty soon he could feel the sweet, fine gathering of pressure deep inside his cods. He held back, increasing the sensation, and in another moment or two it was too much to keep back and the flood commenced to flow.

He clenched his teeth and arched his back and hung in the saddle like a bronc buster getting his teeth loosened after a hard day's night.

Janie screamed and he would have to admit that maybe he grunted and groaned some his own self.

All in all it proved not half so bad an ordeal as he'd feared, by damn.

Afterward, when he reached onto the night stand for a smoke, Janie poked him in the ribs—hard—and said, "Light me one of those things too, cowboy. Then we'll talk while you rest that thing ready for the next tussle."

Longarm was fairly sure he knew just what "thing" it was Janie meant when she said that.

Chapter 15

Janie reached over, he thought in search of a caress. Instead she plucked the freshly lighted cheroot out of his hand and put it between her own somewhat bruised and swollen lips (and how nice it had been getting them that way). He waited a few moments, but she seemed disinclined to relinquish the slim cigar and so he lighted a second one for himself.

She was every bit as sweaty as he was but did not seem to mind in the least. Well, Longarm didn't either now that all the thrashing and banging was ended. In the long run it had all proved pretty much worthwhile, and once he'd solved that initial problem of a nastily slack fit the experience had been a cut or two above the average. Now he was tired. And Janie damn sure had to be. He'd long since lost track of how many times she'd shrieked and gotten her jollies, and likely she hadn't counted either. Both of them, in any event, were entitled to some rest and relaxation at this point.

Janie found the remains of an ancient sardine can that served guests as an ashtray. She set it on the flat of her chest, squarely between her sagging dugs, and invited Longarm to use it.

"Just one thing, honey. If you burn me with that cigar tip, sweetie, I'll think you're starting a whole new sort of playfulness, and you'll have to finish what you start." She winked and added, "There are times, honey, when pain is pleasure too. You hear?"

He could almost believe she meant it. And had no intention of finding out. Better, he thought, to be plenty careful of what happened with the hot ashes off his smoke.

"Do you want to talk now, cowboy?" she offered.

"Hell, woman, I'm not sure I got energy left t' do any talking." He grinned and patted her hip. "But I reckon I can listen if you wanta do the talking."

Janie smiled, obviously feeling that she'd received a compliment, which of course she had, and said, "It's about that ass Norm Colton."

"Yes?"

"It's him you're here to see about, right? I mean, my husband having been a judge I know a little something about jurisdiction. And Norm, he was a federal appointee. Miserable little piece of shit, but federal nonetheless. Which if I remember correctly makes him your responsibility."

"That's right."

"Well, honey, I can tell you right now who killed Norm. For that matter he's the same one who killed Wil Meyers. And while I was downstairs waiting for you, cowboy, I thought I heard someone say somebody else has been killed too. I don't know which of them it was this time. But I know the list his name will be on."

"List?" Longarm asked.

"List," Jane Sproul told him. "There are at least twenty names on the list. And I bet tonight every one of the survivors is hiding under his damned bed, wondering if he will be the next one of those shivarees to die."

Longarm had no idea what the hell she was talking about. But he was willing to listen to whatever it was she wanted to tell him about it.

Chapter 16

"God, I was young then. Pretty too, if I do say so. You aren't following me, are you?"

Longarm shook his head.

"I'm talking about my first wedding, honey."

"First?"

"There've been two actually."

"Not to the judge, you mean now."

"No, this was to a boy . . . isn't that awful, that I think of him as a boy? But then he was, you see. He really was. No, this was just after the war ended."

"Uh huh."

"I was no virgin. I already told you that. But up until then nobody but the men I screwed ever suspected that I played around. And they, if you can believe it, were convinced that they were the first." She laughed and puffed on the cheroot she'd pirated from Longarm. "I guess I lost my cherry five, six times maybe. I got so I was pretty good at squealing and telling the boys how they were too big and oh, it hurt, and oh, it hurt so good, do it again." She chuckled and slapped Longarm on the chest.

"Buddy . . . that was my husband's name . . . well, before he got to be my husband, Buddy came back from the War a genuine hero, you see."

"North or South?" Longarm asked.

"The glorious South, of course. He wouldn't have been a hero if he'd fought for the damn North. Not around here, he wouldn't." She sounded indignant as hell. And like he was mighty dumb to have asked such a question to begin with. Well, maybe she had a point after all, considering that Texas and east Texas in particular had been a mainstay of Southern sentiment and gray-clad manpower.

"Sorry," Longarm said perfunctorily, not particularly meaning it. Shit, he couldn't understand folks who still got excited over affairs long since ended. It just didn't matter. Not any more it didn't.

"Anyway," Janie went on, "Buddy came back this handsome war hero with everyone wanting to kiss his ass, me included." She chuckled some more. "Let me tell you, I was ready to more than just kiss that ass of his. I stuck my tongue in just as far as I could get it. And kissed whatever else of him I could reach too. Oh, he liked that. I showed him things he'd never dreamed of, let me tell you. You should understand that Buddy was kind of . . . innocent, I suppose you'd say. I mean, he'd killed his share of men and then some. But he didn't know squat about women or sex or the really interesting things in life. That was one of the things I liked about him. He was so . . . sincere. Like he only could see one thing at a time. When he was killing people . . . in the War, I mean . . . that's all he thought about. He told me that himself. He never had time to be homesick or think about any of the girls back home or . . . much of anything. He just thought about soldiering and how to kill more damnyankees.

"Then when he got home and went to the gala the town put on in his honor, well, I was there. And like I said, sweetie, I was some kind of fine-looking filly if I do say it myself. These floppy tits you see now? They were just as big then, but they stood tall. Firm and nice. And my belly was flat and my waist tiny wee and my legs shapely. And oh, honey, I did know how to swirl my skirts so my ankles would show and everybody would have sworn it was all an accident that I was too sweet and innocent to so much as be aware of it happening." She laughed and sucked in a drag on her cigar.

"I saw Buddy and he was so popular and good-looking, and I took dead aim on him that night at the dance. Sweetie, it was about as sporting as a farmer taking a hammer to knock a shoat in the head. Buddy never had a chance once I made up my mind that he would be the next man for me to screw.

"What I hadn't counted on was him being so serious and solemn and . . . honorable about the whole thing. Silly son of a bitch. I mean, I can see that now. But at the time, well, at the time I just thought how sweet and dear that was, that he wanted to do right by me and not bring me to any harm. Can you believe it?" She shook her head.

"I mean, honey, I had that boy so worked up he'd shoot come in his drawers every time we had a few minutes alone. He was that horny. But he wouldn't screw me. No, sir. That wouldn't have been proper. He'd finger me plenty and suck my nipples and do most anything else I asked of him. But he wouldn't put his pecker in. Can you imagine? Not even in my mouth. He insisted on keeping his fly buttoned. Kept telling me how much he respected me and how he wanted me to be a virgin on our wedding night. Of course he was years too late for that little event, but I wasn't about to tell *him* that. Hell, if I could lose my cherry half a dozen other times, well, what difference would one more make? Right? So anyway, Buddy was all worked up, and I was too. I mean, he had this tent pole in his drawers that felt damn near as big as that thing of yours, and I sure wanted it, honey. I mean, I wanted that thing to ream me out, hole by hole. And then go back and take seconds. I wanted that boy *bad*."

Longarm had no trouble believing her when she said that. He tapped the ash off his cigar and fluffed the pillow under the back of his neck, giving Janie all the time she wanted to get her tale out.

"So anyway, Buddy wanted to get married. And what the hell, I was willing. I thought I was in love. Never mind that what I was in was rut. What with him refusing to put it in, I was about as horny as he was, and no amount of tongues or fingers or whatever was going to help. What I wanted . . . and what I thought I needed . . . was that handsome boy's cock. So about the tenth or so time he asked me to marry him, I said yes.

"And let me tell you, sweetie, that wedding was the social event of the century." She grinned. "I'm not kidding you. That's what the newspaper called it. Really."

Newspapermen, Longarm thought but carefully did not say, are ofttimes prone to exaggeration.

"Social event of the century, yes indeedy-dee." She laughed, obviously somewhat past the point of believing those long ago printed opinions. "Where was I?"

"You were marrying the local war hero."

"Yes, of course." Janie sighed and looked fairly serious for a change. "Buddy was so . . . sincere. Kind of dumb, of course. I can see that now. But definitely sincere. So anyway, honey, we got married. This was in the late morning, in the Congregational church over on Hood Avenue." She sighed again. "We had a lovely ceremony. Everybody came. I mean everybody. Even the nigger field hands came to crowd close and then line up for molasses and corncakes after. And the reception?" She rolled her eyes.

"There hasn't ever been a reception to equal that one. Not in all the years since. Folks came from four counties, I swear. There were two steers and probably half a dozen full-grown hogs roasted on spits and washtubs of boiled corn and field peas and pies and cakes enough to feed an army . . . a Southern army, of course . . . and heaven knows what-all else. It was something, let me tell you. Tubs of punch for the ladies and something a little stronger for the gents. Which contributed to the troubles, of course, but no one could have thought of that beforehand. Could they?"

Longarm had no idea what she meant. But then he wasn't expected to, so surely the question was a rhetorical one. He puffed on his smoke and let the woman go on.

"Buddy was so handsome. And my gown, let me tell you,

58

honey, I was a real knockout. All dressed up in lace and crin-
olines in the style that was fashionable before the War went
and ruined everything for us. Oh, I was pretty then. Every
man in the crowd was looking at me and seeing how high and
proud my tits were, and I could tell that every one of them
was envying Buddy that night.

"When evening came we cut the cake and had a last dance
and then sneaked away. To the hotel. Not this hotel, mind, but
the old Southern Arms. Can you believe that name? Corny.
But at the time we thought it was a fine, defiant reminder to
the Yankees who came through and had to stay there. At the
time it was the only hotel in Addington, and that is where we
took the honeymoon suite. Of course it hadn't been called the
honeymoon suite until we booked it, but that's what they
named it then. It was on the top floor, which was only the
second floor but even so it was as tall a building as we had
in town barring the public buildings like the courthouse and
City Hall. So anyway, we slipped away to the hotel, and our
suite was all decorated and beautiful and there were flowers
and bowls of fruit and some bubbly champagne that Buddy
never had before, and truth to tell I never had champagne
before that night either, though I've drunk enough since to
take a bath in." She looked away, the movement casual in
appearance although Longarm had the impression that what
Jane Sproul was telling him was of considerable importance
to her, never mind the seemingly easy flow of words. There
was pain lying deep beneath the otherwise light tone of voice.

"Buddy and me . . . I really did think I was in love with
him, and I know he really did think he was in love with me.
And we had the wedding of the goddamn century, didn't we?"

"Yeah," Longarm said. "Yeah, Janie, it for sure was the
wedding of the century, wasn't it?"

She kept her face turned away, but from the side he could
see one small, bright tear rolling down across the wrinkles and
the powder that marred her puffy cheeks. She pretended that
she hadn't shed it, and he pretended that he hadn't seen it.

"Go on," he prompted after some moments of awkward
silence.

"Yeah. Right." She sniffed. "Damn right, honey."

Chapter 17

"It was the liquor, of course. They were drunk. For that matter so was Buddy. And I was too, at least a little bit. Maybe . . ." She shrugged. "Nobody will ever know that, will they?"

"No," Longarm agreed, fairly sure he was on safe ground regardless of what it was she was talking about because actions once taken can never be called back and no one will ever know what might have been but was not.

"We had a cold supper that the hotel laid out for us. Potato salad and fried squab and some cheese and hard sausages. And of course the champagne. It was nice. And Buddy wanted to do things right. Me, I wanted to rip his pants down around his ankles and get to tasting the thing that interested me most, but Buddy wanted to do everything all dignified and proper. And he kept saying that we had all the rest of our lives for that. Ha! What a laugh that turned out to be, sweetie."

"What hap . . . ?"

"You know what a shivaree is, honey?"

"Of course. A bunch of lunatics making noise and raising a ruckus so a pair of newlyweds can't ignore them and jump into bed. O' course as I understand it the original idea was for the partygoers t' wait a while an' then demand t' see the bed sheets so they could look for the red stain that'd prove first that the groom was man enough to bust his bride's cherry an'

second that the girl was a virgin an' still had her cherry there
t' break.''

"Is that so? Damned if I ever knew that part of it, sweetie.
Around here a shivaree is all like the first thing you said. Hell-
raising and meanness and a way to bother the new married
couple.''

"That's what it's mostly turned into. Wasn't that way t' begin with.''

"I wish it'd been that way here. No, I don't . . . hell, I don't
know what I wish. I only know the way it turned out. Maybe
it would have worked. Maybe not. We'll never know that, will
we?''

"No, you won't,'' he assured her.

"Anyway, honey, around here a shivaree is the mean and
stupid kind. And those boys were pretty much drunk, like I
said. Upstairs in the hotel Buddy and me had our supper and
were about to crawl in the sack. Finally. I mean, I was hot
and ready. I was running juice down below my knees from
thinking about getting that big ol' thing inside me. And I know
Buddy was so worked up he was about to bust. Hell, I was
afraid he was going to spend it all in his drawers and not have
any left over for me if he didn't hurry up and get his clothes
off.

"I hurried through the meal as fast as he'd let me and went
into the bedroom to put on something pretty that he could turn
around and take right back off me. You know?''

"I know,'' Longarm said as obviously she wanted him to
contribute something to the conversation.

"I got my gown off and my fluffy night dress on, cut real
low so it showed my tits. I opened the door to call Buddy in
and tell him it was time he should screw my ass off. Or any-
place else he wanted to stick it. And about that time the stupid
shivaree crowd showed up.''

"They got into the room?''

"Oh, hell no. They were outside. But they were loud and
calling out all sorts of comments. You know. Saying things
they were drunk enough to think were funny. And Buddy was

61

drunk enough to feel insulted. Maybe if it hadn't been for the liquor and the champagne . . .'' She sighed once more, and now the tears were flowing freely.

Longarm kept his mouth shut. He didn't think this was any time for him to be intruding on her memories.

"They were our friends. That is the worst thing about it, don't you see. They were all our friends. But they were drunk and they were loud and they were insulting. Not that they meant to be insulting. But they were. And Buddy was so . . . sensitive. So protective of me. He thought I was a real lady, don't you see. He thought I was a virgin and shouldn't be hearing the coarse, awful things they were saying in the shivaree. Sex talk. You know.''

He nodded, but she did not see. She was still looking away although she no longer tried to keep her tears a secret. There was no way she could have done that in any case. She was crying very hard now and very openly.

"Buddy got mad. He opened the window out onto the balcony and cussed them. Of course that only got them worked up all the more. And then someone . . . I don't know who it was . . . got the idea that they should all climb up onto the balcony so they could peek into the bedroom windows. Buddy was furious about that. But some of the drunks started climbing up the porch-roof supports and over the railing onto the balcony while others down below were beating on pots and clanging cowbells and ringing angle irons and the like. I remember hearing a voice call out that Buddy should share, that there was enough to go around and they should all have a piece of what he had. I . . . I think I recognized the voice. I think it was one of the boys I'd been with before. But I couldn't swear to that. Not that it makes any difference, I suppose. But,'' she shuddered, "I think it was Wil Meyers.'' She paused a moment.

"Wil was the . . . third, was it? Third or maybe fourth boy I screwed. Randy was the first, then . . .'' She shook her head. "I think the voice was Wil's.''

"Uh-huh.''

"And some of the others laughed and thought that was funny. Buddy didn't think so. Not at all. And by then some of the boys were climbing onto the balcony. Buddy jumped out the window and grabbed hold of someone . . . Jeremy Baker, I think that was . . . and threw him off the balcony onto the crowd below. Everybody thought that was the funniest thing ever. Then Buddy threw someone else off. I don't recall who that would have been. And that's when it all started to go really bad."

Longarm said nothing, waiting.

"Buddy ran to where Wallace Tatlinger was trying to get over the rail. He punched him in the face. Buddy punched Wallace, that is. And Wallace lost his grip on the rail and fell backward off the balcony. He hit a hitching rail on the street below. Hit right in the small of his back. It was just terrible luck, that's all. He broke his back. Wallace never walked again, not a step. He died, oh, three or four years ago, I think it was. And in all that time he never walked another step nor felt a thing from his waist on down.

"And even that wasn't the worst of it. Some of the boys got mad at Wallace getting hurt. No one knew then how badly he was hurt, but they got mad at Buddy and some started saying mean, awful things and threatening him, and all the while some of the others who weren't so angry or serious were still calling out crude things about me and how big my tits were and how they'd be glad to come up and help Buddy satisfy me and still others were all this while trying to climb up onto the balcony, and Buddy was getting madder and the shivaree boys were getting louder and . . ." She ran out of breath. Or something. And had to stop for a few moments.

"More of them were on the balcony than Buddy could deal with. And he was scared. Afraid the men would hurt me. Afraid he had lost control. I don't know what else. Whatever, he pulled a gun out. I didn't even know he had a gun with him. He had it in a pocket. It was a little thing. It didn't look like much. It had five shots in it. I know that for a fact, you see, because Buddy shot five of the shivaree bunch with that little gun. He'd been in the War and I guess killing didn't mean much to him any more, and he stood there on that balcony and he shot five of his good friends. Just stood there and took aim and shot into them one by one by one. Five shots. Abel Warner was killed outright. Jack Hawkins was hit in the face. He screamed steady for four days before he finally died, and a mercy that was when it happened. Norm Colton was wounded but not badly. So were Pete Nare and Jason Morton.''

Longarm frowned. Of the five men who were shot that long ago night, two died at the time—well, as good as immediately, a couple days hardly mattered, this much later—and two of the remaining three were recent murder victims. As was Wil Meyers who Janie said might have been the first to suggest the shivaree crowd help her new groom with his marital responsibilities. ''You think . . . ?''

''Yes, I do. I most certainly do.''

''But what happened . . . ?''

''Buddy was tried and convicted. He was a hero to the town and wouldn't have been found guilty of anything less. But two boys were dead and another crippled for life and three others wounded. It was too much for the town to forgive. So Buddy was tried and found guilty. As it was, though, he was let off as lightly as the people could stomach. Anyone else would have been hanged. Buddy was sentenced to thirty years in prison. He was . . . earlier this year he was released on parole. Something about good behavior while he was in prison. I don't know. It was in the newspapers. He was let go. That's all I know for sure.''

''Have you heard from him, Janie?''

She shook her head. ''Not for years. I was still young, you know. And my hero, the supposed love of my life, had gone and murdered two men and would be in prison for . . . well, when you're that young, thirty years is the same as a lifetime.''

''You divorced him?''

''That wasn't necessary. I mean, I would have. I've never been one to let myself get bogged down by convention or social expectation. But as it happens, it wasn't necessary. He never bedded me, remember. The shivaree interrupted that. So it was easy to get the marriage annulled. Technically speaking, the wedding of the century never took place. Funny, huh?''

"Yeah," Longarm said dryly. "Funny as shit."

Janie shrugged. "Walker Sproul was the judge who presided over the annulment. He took one look at my tits and decided he would like to have what Buddy didn't get to enjoy. The rest, as they say, is history."

"And now?" Longarm asked.

"Now my first husband . . . well, sort of . . . is out of prison and is going around killing the people who ruined his life. I know that, honey. I know it just as sure as I know I love to screw. Buddy Matthews is the man who murdered Wil Meyers and Norm Colton and now Pete Nare. I promise you he is."

Longarm reached the end of his cheroot and stubbed the butt out in the ashtray that lay on Janie Sproul's ample chest. Her story about the shivaree was sad enough in its way. But her conclusions about the murders, well, he wasn't so sure about that.

Still, it was something he would keep in mind. He would talk to some people, and . . .

Before he could plan any further his eyes went wide with surprise. And then fluttered near closed again once he realized what was going on. Janie had put out her smoke too and laid the ashtray aside.

Now she was down at Longarm's crotch, her tarnished copper hair spread over his lower belly and lightly tickling his balls while her mouth, all warm and wet and eager, sucked and pulled at a cock that, while worn and thoroughly spent, seemed better able to recuperate than he would have suspected.

In fact the blind snake was commencing to stand up and nose around once more under her encouragement.

Well shit, he thought, if she was willing . . .

Chapter 18

Amos, in his guise as the dead postmaster's kin, joined Longarm for a late lunch. Or an early supper. Whatever it was
called, Janie Sproul had kept him out of the dining room for
the duration of the normal dinner hour and then some. Amos
bitched mightily about having been kept waiting for so long
but quieted down when Longarm explained—well, partially;
there were some things about his meeting with the widow
Sproul that he did not pass along to the Ranger—about the
information he'd received.

"You want to know what I think?" Amos asked around a
mouthful of greasy but otherwise tasty pork chop.

"That's why I told it to you, old pard."

"I think the woman is sincere. I mean, you wouldn't accept
her story so readily if you didn't think so, and I trust your
judgment about things like that. But I think it's a case of a
woman's imagination running away with the facts."

"Why's that?" Longarm asked.

"Look, this whole thing has to do with politics, Longarm.
Not revenge. Not some dumb story from out of that poor woman's past. You know how some people think the whole world
revolves around them and anything that happens only happens
because it will affect them. Right?"

"I've knowed folks like that, sure. We all have. But this

66

widow woman . . .'' He shrugged. That just wasn't the way he'd read Janie. Not really.

"Okay, so maybe that's putting it a little too strongly. But you get the general idea of what I'm saying, don't you?''

"I think I do.''

"Good. Because these killings really don't have anything to do with some dim and dusty incident from the past. The reason there is something that she can think is a connection is simple, Longarm. The boys who were being young and silly at the shivaree those years ago were all the young men of their particular generation who grew up here. And quite naturally that same crowd of boys are now grown men. Grown men who run things politically in this town. And who want to run things on a wider scale if they can manage it.''

Longarm raised an eyebrow.

"This crowd in Addington, Custis, is trying to take over the remnants of the old Whig party and turn it into their big chance to make a major move. They call themselves the Texas First party, and by moving into what little is left of the old Whig crowd they have the votes to dominate the Whig organization here in an about five or six other counties in east Texas. It's a sort of leverage. The Whigs have a good share of the influence here. Not quite a majority but almost. I mean, this is kind of a stick-in-the-mud bunch in this area. They don't let go of the past easily. So the Whigs aren't exactly powerful, but they are close to it. And they stick tight. They're well-known for voting as a bloc. Very solid. So by forming a scant majority within the Whig organization and then controlling it, the Texas Firsters have been able to virtually double their influence. Fifty percent plus one and they get the other forty-nine percent as a gift, so to speak. Theirs to do with as they wish. D'you see where I'm going with this?''

"Could be.''

"Of course you do. They figure to take firm root here and then grow like a weed, like a vine taking hold in one spot and pretty soon expanding all around it. If they can get a firm hold here, Longarm, next they'll have a voice in the state capital.

Senate, House of Representatives, state supreme court, wherever they can get a toehold. And that is all entirely legal. Don't get me wrong. My boss has no grief with anything they do that's legal and aboveboard. So long as the Texas First party members are elected fair and square, we'll do everything we can to protect them and to guarantee their rights. Unfortunately, there are rumors . . . which now look to be something more than rumors . . . about their methods for gaining control of some political offices.''

"Norman Colton, you mean?''

"It's possible. Colton wasn't a Texas Firster. His appointment to office came out of Washington, you know. And he was loyal to his party. Just like Pete Nare was loyal to his party. Which was the opposition to the current administration but there again he was no Texas Firster.''

"And the first man who was killed? What was his name again?''

"Meyers. Wil Meyers.''

"Right. Thanks.''

"Anyway, you asked about Meyers' political affiliation,'' Amos reminded him. "The truth is that I don't know. I haven't wanted to be too nosy about the other murders. I can safely bring up anything relating to my so-called cousin Norman, but I didn't want to tip my hand about Meyers. Now, of course, it looks like there's a pattern beginning to show so I'll be free to ask around some more. But still as a concerned relative. I'll leave the official investigating to you since you're out in the open about it.''

Longarm nodded. "And your boss in the Rangers thinks the Texas First party is beginning to have some influence inside the Rangers, I take it?''

That was the wrong thing to say, he saw immediately: the open friendliness in Amos's eyes was instantly replaced by a veil of—at the very least—caution.

"The Rangers don't get involved in politics, Deputy. Never!''

"No, I reckon you don't," Longarm said quickly. But it sounded lame even to him.

Of course Amos's anger was more than answer enough. Damn right the head man in Austin was afraid that this Texas First crowd was trying to influence law enforcement as well as put their people into elected office.

And when someone started trying to take that kind of control, well, any sensible citizen would tend to open his eyes and his ears wider than usual and prepare to defend the rights his government was supposed to guarantee for him.

"D'you, uh, want a piece o' pie t' go with that," Longarm suggested in a peace-making effort.

"If you're buying, sure," Amos said, accepting the unspoken apology in the spirit Longarm intended.

Chapter 19

It was no trick to find out where the latest murder took place. A large sign painted in bright red lettering proclaimed the location of Nare and Son, Hardware and Farm Implements, Offered to the Gen'l Public at Wholesale Price.

The two-story building was perhaps twenty feet wide but ran the full depth of the city lot, which was a good seventy or eighty feet or so. According to what Longarm had overheard earlier in the police chief's office, the top floor was given to living quarters and the ground floor to business. There was an alley running along the east side of the building, and that would be where the door was, the one Peter Nare opened to find a gun staring him in the face.

Naturally enough the store remained closed after the proprietor's death. If there was family left to take over the business, they would not likely do so until after a suitable mourning period. The top-floor windows, at least those that could be seen from the street, were closed, and there was no way for Longarm to tell if anyone was there. Seeing no policemen in the vicinity he assumed the chief was already in possession of whatever information was available. If any.

Longarm figured there was at least a strong likelihood that this killing and the two previous ones, including that of federal employee Norman Colton, were connected. So it was within his jurisdiction to make inquiries into the death of Pete Nare.

He stood on the board sidewalk across the street from the empty and somewhat forlorn-looking hardware store and lighted a cheroot while he took a look up and down the block.

There was a saloon on the corner, normally the most likely source of information about any happening in the neighborhood. But Longarm had been in the place the previous day and found only silent hostility there.

He smiled when he saw, tucked between a hatmaker and a haberdashery, a small storefront that announced itself as an ice cream parlor and confectioner. Perfect. He stayed where he was until he finished his smoke, then ambled down the block toward the ice cream parlor. A midafternoon sweet sounded just about right.

Longarm was not sure if he should feel like a cockerel in a roost full of hens. Or a turd floating in the punch bowl.

For sure he was the only male in sight. Unless you counted those visible through the glass front as commerce passed by the tiny island of feminism.

The proprietress and staff were exclusively female and so was the afternoon clientele. Save, that is, for one tall, lean United States deputy marshal.

The woman who seemed to be in charge of the parlor was perhaps fifty or so, with hair like steel, eyes like ball bearings and a build that suggested she could wrestle steers and not give much away in terms of raw power. She had two waitresses, both young women in their late teens or early twenties, each wearing identical uniforms of white shirt, gray skirt and an overblouse (or whatever the glorified aprons might be called) made of pink fabric with huge ruffles at the arm holes and embroidered lettering on the left breast to indicate the girl's name—Barbara being a short girl with a round face, dimples, and brown hair tied back in a severe bun and Clarice being tall, slim, and almost pretty except for a large wart on the side of her nose that gave her the unfortunate appearance of a Halloween witch illustration come to life.

The patrons—the little store was nearly full—were ladies in various degrees of finery taking time out from the taxing chores of shopping, pausing here for refreshment so they would be able once more to contribute to the economy of their town.

Married women all, he was sure. He could tell by the piles of bundles, sacks, and parcels spread out on the floor near their feet. Women would spend so freely only if someone else was providing the wherewithal. Or so Longarm believed. He supposed he could be in error about that since it was only one man's lifetime of experience that led him to the assumption.

Whatever, they were a handsome sight, this gathering of Addington's grandest dams at the—well, sort of—watering hole.

"Yes, sir?" The voice was tentative, unsure and a trifle too high-pitched. It was Clarice who'd lost out and had to wait on the male in their midst.

"You have ice cream, the sign says?"

"Yes, sir. Seven flavors." She pointed toward a sign high on the back wall listing the assortment.

"Vanilla will be fine," he said.

"Yes, sir. We have some nice fresh dewberries. Would you like some on top?"

"Please."

She gave him a smile that seemed genuine, dipped into a minimal curtsy and swept away with the hem of her skirt flying up a bit to reveal an ankle that was not half bad. If it weren't for that wart . . .

Longarm removed his Stetson and looked around, but there was no provision made for gentlemen's hats here. He settled for putting it on the seat of the other chair at his tiny table.

The ladies at the other tables had virtually stopped talking when he entered, but by now they were beginning to relax in his presence—if not actually forgetting about him then at least no longer finding it unnatural for him to be there among them in what he now strongly believed was normally an exclusive preserve of the fair gender.

Clarice came back with a fluted dish of ice cream so rich with cream and sugar that it was more yellow than white, what he could see of it beneath a thick overlay of those dark, plump berries so like blackberries except for their lighter, sweeter, more delicate flavor. Longarm hadn't had dewberries in . . . he tried to think back and failed to come up with so much as an approximation . . . years. A good many years.

"Would you like coffee with that, sir? Or some cookies? We have some nice sugar cookies."

"Sugar cookies would be good. And tea, not coffee." He managed to keep from snickering into his sleeve. Sugar cookies and tea. Shee-it. Still, it would smooth out any lingering rough edges. After that, the ladies, any who bothered to pay attention, would think of him as just another of the girls and never mind appearances.

Yes, sirree bob. Ice cream, cookies and a spot of tea. Just what every he-man needs for his afternoon break.

Longarm sat back with his expression blank. And his ears wide, wide open.

Chapter 20

"Nope. Pete Nare didn't have no family. Nobody you can talk to, else I wouldn't be saying anything in answer to your question, by God, and that's a fact. Word is that your name is Mud around here. But I don't suppose there's anything wrong with telling you there's nothing for you to look into when it comes to Pete. He was married once, but that was, oh, a good many years back. Married Normajean Banfrey from downriver. Her father . . . he's dead too now . . . farmed some, ran a catfish trotline, got by if you know what I mean. Anyhow, Pete married Normajean, but she up and died. In childbirth. That was a long time back. Ever since then Pete pretty much kept to himself. Stopped by here every Saturday night after closing and had him two shots, never any more, then went over to Fat Nell's to get his ashes hauled. Regular as an eight-day clock, Pete was. But no family. You're wasting your time."

"I thank you anyhow, neighbor," Longarm said, knocking back a straight shot of rye whiskey—Pennsylvania distilled, which made it second-best but not actually bad—to help cut the cloying sweetness of all the ice cream and pastries and shit he'd just waded through over at the ice cream parlor. Or make that ladies' social. Either one seemed to fit well enough.

"Another?" the bartender asked.

"No, that will do me for the moment. But don't bust the

bottle quite yet. I expect I'll be back for seconds later on.''

"Your money is welcome enough, Marshal. Just don't ask me no more questions, all right?''

"You do overwhelm a fella with hospitality around here, don't you," Longarm offered.

"Just being honest, Marshal. Just being honest with you.''

"I guess I'm s'posed to appreciate that.'' Longarm gave the barkeep a grin and a wink. "Or something.''

The barman shrugged and busied himself polishing an already spotless patch of brightwork along the edge of the long bar.

Longarm dropped a dime on the shiny surface and ambled out onto the street.

He knew right good and well where he needed to go next.

"Mrs. Allard?'' The woman he spoke to was pale and thin, with brown hair gathered in a sweat-moistened clump at the back of a long and rather elegant neck. Had she been dressed in something nicer than a shapeless housedress she might have been fairly attractive. As it was, she looked worn-out and haggard from too much work, too many children, and too little money.

"What is it you want, mister?'' Her voice was full of suspicion. Possibly with good reason, judging from the snide and catty things Longarm had heard about her husband.

"Are you Sylvie Allard?''

"Maybe I am, maybe I'm not.''

Longarm shrugged and produced his wallet, opening the fold to display his badge. He decided no good purpose would be served by giving Mrs. Allard a lecture on the niceties of legal jurisdiction.

"Oh.'' She tugged at her dress where the waist should have been as if in a futile attempt to make herself a trifle more presentable in the face of duly constituted authority.

"Are you Mrs. Sylvie Allard, ma'am?'' Longarm persisted.

"Yes. That is . . . I am. Sir.''

"I need to ask you a few questions, ma'am.''

"About what, officer?"

"Peter Nare."

"I don't . . . that is, I do know . . . I mean I did know Peter, I mean Mr. Nare. Of course. I've known Mr. Nare about all my life. As long as I can remember, you see. But I don't know anything about him. Not really."

Longarm stepped past Sylvie Allard, just inside the door to her home, and glanced around to see if anyone might be able to overhear. Satisfied that they were alone at least for the moment at the front of the house, he turned back to her and in a low voice said, "You and me can have a quiet talk now, Miz Allard, one that won't go anywhere but between the two of us. Or I can leave now an' get a warrant. Come back an' search your home for clues. Ask your husband about the relationship you an' Pete Nare had . . ."

"But I swear to you, Officer, I've never had any sort of rela . . ."

"Monday, Wednesday an' Friday, Miz Allard. Noon to along about two, sometimes three in the afternoons. While your kids was in school or else playing with their cousins over on Water Oak Street when school wasn't in session. You want me t' talk with your husband about what was happening those times, Miz Allard?" It was a cheap shot and Longarm did not feel good about it. He told himself there was no real harm done because he would not say anything about the affair, not to George Allard or anyone else in Addington, Texas, no matter what Sylvie Allard said or did in response.

What the woman did was turn chalky white. He'd thought she was pale before. Shit, he hadn't known then what pale could really look like. Now he did.

He reached out and took her by the elbow to steady her. "Are you all right, ma'am?"

"I . . . yes, I suppose so. Not that you care, damn you." She gave him a dark, darting glare. Which he conceded he fully deserved.

"I'm sorry," he said, meaning it sincerely. "I know this must be a difficult time for you. I mean . . . someone close to you has been murdered and you don't even have the freedom to grieve. Please understand, ma'am. I am interested in finding the man who killed Peter Nare and bringing that man to justice." He cleared his throat. "If that helps any."

Mrs. Allard opened her mouth to say something but was interrupted by a rattle of small feet on the loose planks of the flooring in her rickety-rackety ramshackle house. A herd of small children came shrieking and galloping past, followed a moment later by a slightly younger and plumper version of Sylvie Allard. A sister, no doubt.

"I'm sorry, sir. I am simply not interested in buying your product," Sylvie said in a slightly overloud voice. In a whisper she added, "I have to do my grocery shopping later this afternoon, officer. Can I meet you in the park? In half an hour? Near the teeter-totters beside the river. Please?"

Longarm nodded and tipped his hat, first to Mrs. Allard and then to the other barefoot young woman who had finished giving unheeded orders to the children and who now was drifting toward the pair in the open doorway, her curiosity blatant and unapologetic. "Sorry, ma'am. An' to you too, miss. You ladies have a fine day now, hear?"

He replaced the Stetson firmly on his head and backed politely off the porch before turning and striding purposefully away.

The question now was whether Sylvie Allard would keep her word and meet him in the park.

But then considering the way he'd gone and blackmailed the poor woman, yeah, he figured he could count on seeing her there.

Chapter 21

She was late. Or not coming. Dammit! He angrily ground a cheroot butt out underfoot, then paced back and forth close by the teeter-totter.

"Hey, mister."

He looked up. It was a kid, maybe eight, ten years old—a small boy wearing miniature bib overalls and worn-out shoes three sizes too large. Kid had an older brother, Longarm guessed. "Yeah, son?"

"Get on the other end, please?" The kid pointed to the far end of the teeter-totter, a device damn near impossible to enjoy by oneself.

"What the *fu* . . ." Oh hell, why not? It had been a rather long time. But Longarm managed to remembered how the stupid things worked. He straddled the two-by-eight slab of wood, sitting fairly close to the balance point so as to make the kid's weight about even with his when the laws of leverage applied themselves, and he and the scruffy kid were bouncing up and down like that when Sylvie Allard showed up.

"Am I interrupting anything?" she asked.

"Yeah, you are. An' I thank you for it too." He beckoned the boy over to him and handed the kid a dime. "Go get yourself some ice cream," he said, figuring he still owed the ladies at the ice cream parlor something, considering. Besides, it would get the kid out of earshot.

"Thanks, mister. Thanks a *lot*." The boy charged off like a coyote after a jackass rabbit, and Longarm and the woman drifted down toward the riverbank where the dark water swirled and gurgled over some white, flat rocks.

"I was commencing to think you weren't coming," Longarm admitted.

"I almost didn't, actually." She hesitated. "Would you really tell my husband?"

He shook his head. "No, I reckon not."

That elicited a small smile. "I didn't think you would. Not really."

"But you came anyway."

"You said something that made me come."

"Not that stupid threat about . . ."

"No. What you said was that you want to find the man who killed Peter."

"And your local law?"

"They will want the killing to stop, of course. But they will only charge and convict anyone if he proves to be . . ."

"Convenient?" Longarm suggested.

"Yes. Thank you. That is a nice way to put it."

"Everyone seems t' think politics is already involved in these killings," Longarm said.

"Yes, of course. We are very political around here, you know. Ever since those damn carpetbaggers came in after the War and we didn't know how to defend ourselves from them. Well, we learned. Perhaps too well, if you see what I mean."

"Yeah, I s'pose I do, sort of."

"Yes, well, it is true that Peter was county secretary of the Whig party. There was talk about running him for state office too. In the party, I mean. Peter was a very quiet man. He never wanted the public exposure that holding elective office would have required." She dropped her eyes, and he thought she might even have blushed a little. "He always said he didn't want to take on anything that would mean moving away from Addington."

"He must have loved you very much," Longarm said, in response more to her demeanor than to what she was saying.

The remark hit home. Tears began to slide, silent and unheeded, down her cheeks. She pretended not to notice so he did too.

"Will you even be able to attend the funeral?" he asked.

Sylvie Allard shook her head. "My husband would wonder why. I can't have that."

"No, of course not."

"I am not a bad woman, Officer."

"No, I'm sure you aren't."

She gave him a sharp look. "I mean it, Officer. Appearances to the contrary."

"I meant it too, ma'am." Which was not entirely true, but what the hell. "Can we get back to Peter Nare and the reasons why someone might have wanted him dead?"

"I don't suppose you know about our local politics," she said.

"Not much, no."

"There is a group, old residents mostly, old families here, who want to take over the Whig party and make it into something of their own. Peter opposed them. I think it is more than possible that someone from this new faction could have murdered him to make way for someone of their own choosing in Peter's office."

"These people would feel so strongly about it?"

"Some of them might," she answered.

"Could you give me any names? Not as an accusation, of course. I realize you would have no way to know for sure. But some names for me to look into."

"James Deel, Cory Johnston, Paul Burkett . . ." She hesitated again. "Chief Bender." The police chief's name came out in a bare whisper. She sounded frightened, he thought. Damn.

"You're very brave," he said. "Thank you."

"I'm not brave, Officer. I just . . . don't much give a damn any longer. You know?" She raised her small shoulders and

80

dropped them again. "I only had one small measure of happiness. Now that has been taken away from me. I don't suppose . . ." She didn't finish the thought. And he did not ask.

After a moment Longarm coughed lightly into his fist and changed the subject. "I've heard the possibility mentioned, ma'am, that these killings could have something to do with the shenanigans at a shivaree years back. Revenge for what happened that night."

"A shivaree, Officer?"

"Yeah, they're . . ."

"I know what a shivaree is, of course. The young men around here do it all the time. I remember on our wedding ni . . ." She blushed, stopped, reconsidered bringing that night up.

Longarm, got the distinct impression, though, that Sylvie Allard had been a more than willing bride. Whatever went wrong between herself and her husband happened long after their fondly remembered wedding night. Shivaree and all.

"What I meant to say, Officer, is that I can't think of any reason why anyone would have particularly strong feelings about an ordinary little thing like a shivaree."

"You don't remember a man named Buddy Matthews or someone called Wallace Tatlinger?"

"I remember Wallace, of course. He was such a nice man. A cripple. He died a while back. Who was the other man you named?"

"Matthews," Longarm repeated. "Buddy Matthews."

Mrs. Allard frowned. Then her brow smoothed as memory came to her and she said, "Of course. I'd forgotten. I was a little girl then. There was a scandal. A shooting or something like that, and I think he was sent to prison. But my, that was years and years ago. I'm sure everyone has forgotten all about that by now. We have other things on our minds here, Officer, things more important than old scandals."

"Yes, of course. I, uh, think you were gonna tell me some more about those fellows you mentioned a minute ago, Chief Bender and Deel, Johnston, Burkett?"

"Was I really?"

He smiled at her. "Well, I was kinda hoping."

She glanced toward the sun, which was dropping low on the horizon.

"Just another couple minutes," he asked. "Then I'll try an not bother you no more. And . . . no more threats. I'm sorry 'bout that. I feel badly for doing it."

"Yes, all right. I suppose a few more minutes won't hurt. And then," she straightened her shoulders and tried on a brave but artificial and decidedly strained little smile, "then I shall have to think about my memories, shan't I, as they will be the only things I can look forward to for the rest of my life."

A couple more years, Longarm figured, and Sylvie Allard would, at least in her own mind, be a regular martyr. Thank goodness that wouldn't be on his plate of things to fret about. He had enough worries of his own without taking hers on to boot.

"You were gonna say . . . ?" he prompted.

"Yes, of course. Let's see now. James Deel is . . ."

Chapter 22

Longarm had supper at a small cafe where they either didn't recognize him or were too interested in food to bother deviling the intruder. Whatever the truth, no one treated him like anything but just another customer.

After the meal he lingered over pie and coffee, then lighted a smoke before venturing out onto the streets. It had come dark while he was eating, and Addington—modern though its residents seemed to think it—had no gas lights on the street corners like Denver and San Francisco and other up-to-date metropolises could boast.

It also seemed that Addington closed its doors early. The only lights in the business district were those of the saloons, and Longarm was not interested at the moment in being the object of whispers and stares. Better, he figured, to head back to the hotel for the evening.

Besides, if Amos—uh, Lester Colton hereabouts, and he damn well better remember that before he slipped up and gave Amos away—wanted to see him about anything, it would be at the hotel where contact could be made.

The way he and Amos figured it, Norm Colton's cousin would have no qualms about talking with a federal peace officer. Far from it, in fact. And from Longarm's point of view, Cousin Lester would be one of the very few folks in

Addington willing to talk with him. So there was no harm in the two being seen together. It should seem only natural to the locals and should in fact support Amos's false identity.

Smoking contentedly on a good cheroot, Longarm wandered down the sidewalk toward the hotel.

As he approached the Nare and Son hardware—Peter apparently was the Son indicated there as he had no surviving children of his own—Longarm's gaze was naturally drawn in that direction.

He stopped, hand halfway to his mouth and his lips already parted to receive the soggy end of his cigar.

There might not be much for light at street level, but there damn sure was a light behind one of the windows on the second floor of the murder victim's store.

Someone was moving around inside there, carrying what looked to be a candle instead of a lamp.

But Pete Nare had no living kin. He'd lived alone. And at this time of night there was no sensible reason for anyone to be inside the living quarters over top of the hardware.

It crossed Longarm's mind that Sylvie Allard could have had reason to sneak inside. To recover love notes, perhaps, or other mementos of the long-standing affair between her and Nare.

She might be interested for reasons of sweet sentiment. Or as likely it would be to keep her husband from finding out that he was wearing a cuckold's horns.

On the other hand . . .

Longarm tossed the butt of his cheroot into the street and moved swiftly across the open expanse and into the shadows.

His hand automatically sought the reassuring presence of the big double-action Colt that rode as always in its crossdraw rig just to the left of his belt buckle.

Not that he was expecting trouble exactly. But a man never knows. And he did not know for certain sure that it was Sylvie Allard upstairs in that otherwise dark building, did he?

84

He felt his way back through the alley that ran beside Nare's building and found the doorway where Nare had died roughly twenty-four hours earlier.

It occurred to Longarm that if Nare opened the door facing into this alley and was himself standing in the light inside he would have had no night vision whatsoever and therefore may well never have seen the man who shot him dead.

A fellow should at least be allowed to know why he was being killed, surely.

But then, shit, life is not fair to begin with and death is even less so.

Longarm tried the door and found it unlocked. Closed but not locked. From the outside no one would notice a thing amiss.

Careful to make no sound, Longarm slipped inside and eased the door shut behind him.

He felt his way up the staircase, keeping close to the side wall where there was less likelihood of stepping on a loose, squeaking board that would give him away.

He moved up the stairs slowly. A few inevitable bumps and squeals occurred, but he knew they were quiet enough that the only one apt to notice was himself. To him, of course, they sounded pretty much akin to the noise of a bass drum marching down the boulevard on a Fourth of July afternoon. To anyone else they would likely seem no more than the normal creaks and groanings that every building makes at night.

He reached the top of the stairs.

And didn't know which goddamn way to go next.

That is, he knew which general direction he wanted.

But he'd never been inside the place before and had no idea how it was laid out. It was something he could have asked Sylvie earlier but simply hadn't thought to. Dammit.

And there was no longer any candle flame to be seen, at least not back here where he was. Either whoever was in the place had extinguished the light or there was a door closed between the stairwell and the candle because for sure no light from it intruded here.

Longarm pondered his options.

If he blundered around in this deep, stygian space he was sure as hell gonna trip over something, bump into something, some way make a racket that would scare the shit out of whoever else was up here, which would certainly do Longarm no good.

Or he could risk a light of his own.

What the hell, he reasoned. If he couldn't see the other guy's candle then the other guy couldn't see his match.

And, really, Longarm was pretty well convinced by now that the nocturnal intruder almost had to be Sylvie Allard.

Longarm didn't want to frighten or to embarrass her. He certainly did not want to expose her secrets to the town.

For a moment he considered leaving as silently as he had come, just getting out so that she would never know he had caught onto her search.

But then, he didn't know for certain-sure, did he, that it was Mrs. Allard who was up here.

Better, he decided, to strike a match and get his bearings.

Then he could sneak forward through the place and look to see that it was indeed Mrs. Allard. Once he was satisfied as to that, he decided, he would slide on out again. She would never have to know that he'd come up and checked on her.

As soon as his decision was made, Longarm dipped a thumb and forefinger into the vest pocket where he kept his matches.

He brought out a sulfur-tipped lucifer and used a thumbnail to snap it afire.

The result was somewhat more than he'd anticipated.

No sooner had the flame burst alive, surrounding him with a glare of yellow light, than he heard a roar of surprise.

Definitely a man's deep voice.

And half heard, half saw a bulky form launching itself from somewhere to the left, from the direction away from where he

86

had seen the candlelight minutes earlier.

Shit, apparently whoever was up here finished what he wanted and was feeling around in the dark, either looking for something else or hunting for the stairs so he could leave. Or whatever.

Longarm really didn't have time to ponder it.

Not right then.

He heard a bellow of shock and of challenge.

Sensed the looming presence of another person.

Felt a shoulder drive hard into his lower ribs.

The breath was thumped out of him, and he crashed sideways into a wall, rebounding off it and losing his footing.

He felt something hard and bony—a shin, he thought later—connect with his shoulder and something else—a boot, maybe—hit the side of his face.

There was another yelp, this one of fear more than anything, and the loud clatter of someone taking a fall down the dark stairs.

"Jesus!" a voice called.

Very sensible, Longarm thought. Nobody else was likely to help. Not in a mess like this.

His shoulder felt numb, the side of his face stung like he'd been slapped by six or seven hefty women one right after another, and he couldn't breathe.

Other than that, he was doing okay.

He heard the thumping and bumping continue all the way to the bottom of the stairwell. There was some more crashing about down there and then the sound of a door slamming shut.

Ah well, Longarm thought.

So much for the notion that Mrs. Allard stopped by on a mission of sweet sentiment.

He stayed sitting on the floor—it would have been more comfortable if Peter Nare had invested in some carpet—until he got his breath, then once more found a match to light his way, this time finding a lamp and getting the thing aflame so he could make a proper search of things.

One thing at a time, he thought, and all in due and proper order.

First he would take his own little look-see through the dead man's quarters.

Then the right thing undoubtedly would be for him to notify the local authorities that party or parties unknown had been diddling about in the dark of night.

Chapter 23

The problem, of course, was that he had no idea what he was looking for. If anything. Or where it might be, whatever the hell *it* was.

Whatever, he found nothing of interest. So maybe the intruder found what he came for and was on his way out when Longarm blundered into the middle of things. Dammit.

Eventually concluding that he was accomplishing nothing beyond a waste of time, Longarm called a local cop.

He did so by the simple expedient of raising a window sash over the main street and perching on the sill with a cheroot at a jaunty angle until the night-shift officer wandered by. Longarm hailed the fellow from above, startling him only slightly, and that was that.

Or that should have been that.

In retrospect it seemed a helluva lot more bother than it was worth, because for the next two hours he was stuck in Peter Nare's apartment being grilled by a very unhappy Chief J. Michael Bender.

"Look, dammit, for the . . . what is this, the sixth time? seventh? however many . . . I'm telling you I saw a light moving up here an' remembered hearing that this Nare fella didn't have any kin. So I got curious. An' I didn't want the robber t' get away. Dammit, man, I am a peace officer my own self, y'know. So I came up for a look-see. An' then . . . well, hell, I been through all this so many times b' now you should have the story memorized.''

"And you say you called my officer immediately afterward?''

"That's what I told you,'' Longarm declared, certain that the only one who was in a position to dispute him would be the robber he'd disturbed in the place. No one else would have any possible way to know when he had entered Nare's quarters or how long he had stayed.

And, shit, it wasn't like it was an important lie anyhow. He really hadn't found anything of interest here.

"You didn't look around at all?''

"Not more'n to see was anyone still inside. I lit the lamps an' gave the place a quick look-through, then went an' set in that window till your man come by. That couldn't have been more than, oh, a couple-three minutes. Tops.''

"You didn't take anything while you were waiting?''

"Search me if you want. I said I didn't.''

The Addington police chief acted like he was giving some serious thought to that offer but in the end stopped short of expressing his hostility quite that openly.

Then, dammit, the sawed-off Ranger sergeant George Braxton showed up, and Longarm had to go through the whole story again for his benefit.

When Longarm was done reciting, Braxton and Bender went off into a corner to confer. Longarm, under the watchful eye of the night cop, went into a different corner to sulk a mite and to smoke.

Or anyway to sulk so far as the young night copper was concerned.

What he was actually doing was looking for a spot where sound carried particularly well.

And he found it.

Even though Bender and the tame Ranger were whispering softly between themselves, it was no great strain for Longarm to overhear the gist of the conversation.

According to Bender, the drawers to Nare's desk were unlocked. Hell, Longarm could confirm that. He had checked. But then he also knew there was nothing of any particular interest or importance in any of those desk drawers.

What he hadn't know—and what Chief Bender was telling the Ranger now—was that there *should* have been certain articles in those now innocent drawers.

Official records and minute books of the local Whig party, for instance.

Longarm remembered now that Peter Nare had been secretary of the party.

Now, according to the police chief, all those records were missing.

It occurred to Longarm that if the Texas First people wanted to alter the past, this would be a perfect opportunity for them to do so.

Because with no records to prove otherwise, the party leadership could claim virtually anything they wanted, right down to new directions as determined by closed caucus vote.

Which would pretty much play into the hands of the people Amos and his chief in Austin were worried about.

Interesting, Longarm thought.

He stood in his corner quietly puffing on his cheroot and letting his ears flap in the breeze—well, sort of—until Bender and Braxton got done with their own private—or so they thought—little caucus and finally allowed that he could be dismissed.

"Yes, and, um, thank you for, uh, trying to help out," Bender said without any great amount of graciousness. "Next time, though, you might want to call on my people first. Our jurisdiction, you know. And besides, all of my people are trained officers. None of us would have let the intruder get by."

Yeah. Right. Longarm didn't say anything, though. Hell, if the locals wanted to start thinking of him as a blithering idiot, that was just fine by him. After all, no one is afraid of a clown. Let them think whatever they liked.

"G'night, chief. Sergeant." He tipped his hat just polite as pie and got the hell outa there before he went and said something that might tip them that Billy Vail made his appointments on the basis of ability and not politics.

Chapter 24

Longarm was about half-asleep, drowsing on the thin edge of it, when he heard a thin scratching, the sort of sound that might be made by a wire lockpick.

So much for sleep.

He came fully awake, the familiar heft of the Colt butt in his hand as he sat upright and cocked his head to one side to listen all the more closely.

It wasn't a lockpick he could hear scratching at the door but something . . . a cat maybe? Not the door at all but maybe a mouse in the ceiling or a wall? Or possibly fingernails? Damned if it didn't sound like someone scratching on the door, all right.

"Psst!"

Longarm grinned and went barefoot to unbolt, unlock, and unlatch the thing. As a precaution, however, he kept the revolver in his hand. Hey, he'd been wrong that one time way back when he'd thought he had made an error but of course had not. Or so he sometimes liked to claim.

"That you, Amos?"

"Shit no, it's me, Lester Colton."

"Right, Lester." Longarm pulled the door open and let Amos inside. "What's that you're carrying?"

"We drank yours last night. My turn tonight." He held a

dark brown bottle aloft, as if to display a trophy.

"You're a sneaky little sumbish, but sometimes you get it right in spite o' yourself," Longarm said.

Amos chuckled and uncorked the bottle. Which proved to be a corn whiskey instead of a rye. But what the hell. A man can't have everything. Which is no reason to stop trying, of course. "Cheers."

"Mud in your eye."

Both took deep pulls from the bottle, passing it back and forth until the edge was off. Then Longarm motioned Amos to the chair and took a seat on the side of the bed. "Hear anything t'day?"

"Just that the police chief doesn't like you worth a damn. He doesn't really believe that story you gave him about passing by and seeing a light in Nare's living quarters."

"How'd you hear about that?"

"It's all over town by now, jumping from saloon to saloon. Deliberate, of course. They want to make sure nobody in town has anything to do with you. Making you out to be a liar is just a part of that."

"Reckon that makes sense after a fashion." Longarm smiled. "And o' course Bender wouldn't believe my story. After all, it's the truth."

"Really?"

"Uh huh." Longarm gave Amos a somewhat more complete account of the affair than Chief Bender had gotten.

"The son of a bitch was after the party's records," Amos said.

"That's what it looks like."

"I wonder what was in them that was so important, the party secretary was killed just to get them," Amos mused.

"If there's a connection."

"If?" Amos challenged. "There pretty much has to be a connection."

"Maybe so, maybe no. Could be someone was just taking advantage of an opportunity that fell into his lap. Or o' course it could be that Nare was killed for those records, like you say. But if the killer was after the records, why not grab them last night instead o' this evening?''

''A gunshot sounds mighty loud to the fellow who's pulling the trigger. He couldn't have known no one would hear the shot last night.''

''No, but he coulda watched from across the street or something. That's what I'd of done.''

''Our man might not be as cool about murder as you, my friend,'' Amos suggested.

''He's had his practice lately, it looks like.''

''Still and all . . .''

Longarm sighed. ''One thing you can count on when it comes to criminals.''

''What's that?''

''They're all of them crazy as hell an' about as predictable as the weather.''

''Isn't that the natural truth.'' Amos had another go at the bottle, then handed it to Longarm.

''Someday, ol' son, I'm gonna teach you about drinkin' whiskey,'' Longarm said, taking a long swallow of the mellow corn and returning the jug to his friend.

''In the meantime I thought you might wanta hear something that came up in conversation this afternoon.''

''What's that?''

''One of the Texas First boys was kind of pumping me to see could I offer any support for them in my home county. You know?''

''That sounds normal enough.''

''Yeah, but wait until you hear what this guy was hinting at.''

''Just hinting?''

''It isn't the sort of thing you come right out and say. Not unless you know the other person mighty well.''

''And . . . ?''

Amos lowered his voice a bit even though they were undoubtedly alone and beyond any serious likelihood of eavesdropping. "You know that rescission clause in the Texas constitution?"

"The who-what?"

Amos smiled and shook his head. "I can tell you're no Texan."

"Thank goodness there's at least one regular human in this room," Longarm returned.

"When Texas came into the Union back in the forties, my friend, one of the privileges we kept for ourselves was the right to withdraw from the Union if we damn well wanted."

"Which I think was overruled by the highest court possible a few years back. The court of shot an' shell. In case you ain't heard, Tex, the South lost."

"Yes, but the provision is still there, still in force."

"Still there maybe but not in force."

"Yes, well, there is room for doubt, isn't there?"

"Not the way I understand it."

"But then you aren't a member of the Texas First party, are you."

"C'mon. You mean that? These dumb assholes actually think they can take Texas out of the Union and create their own country again? Has anyone reminded them that it didn't work the last two times they tried it?"

"Two? Oh. You mean when we seceded from Mexico and then again . . ."

"Yeah. Two. And it didn't work worth a damn neither time."

"That's the way you see it, but don't forget that it's Texans we're talking here. And we can be stubborn sons of bitches when we take a notion to."

"So they're really thinking about trying it again, huh."

"By legal writ, not by force of arms, I think," Amos said.

"But if a few folks had t' die to make it all possible . . ."

Amos shrugged. "I couldn't say that for sure, of course. But when you think about it . . ."

Longarm sat in silence for a moment, then said, "Y'know, Amos, one o' these days I'm gonna be sent out on a case that's simple an' straightforward and don't involve a damn thing other than a little robbery, murder, stuff like that. You know. *Easy* stuff.''

"I keep hoping for the same sort of thing," Amos said, handing the whiskey bottle to Longarm after taking a quick one for himself. "It never happens. But I do keep hoping."

Chapter 25

Longarm's morning was something less than fruitful. There were three murder victims now whose families he should have interviewed in search of a common link or bond among them that might account for their having been killed.

That, at least, was the theory.

Except as he already knew, Peter Nare had no surviving family, his wife and only child having died together in child-birth some years previous.

As for Norman Colton, whose murder brought him here, it turned out that the Addington postmaster, although a native of the community himself, had married a girl from Tennessee, and according to Colton's neighbors, the distraught widow had left for an extended visit with her family soon after the funeral. Exactly when, or even if, she intended to return to Texas was unclear, though one busybody biddy of a neighbor was at least helpful enough to volunteer Longarm the Tennessee address where he could interview Mrs. Colton if he so desired. He'd told her he would get back to her on that if need be.

And as for the first man killed, Wil Meyers, he turned out to have a family, a wife, and a regular rat pack of runny-nosed children. But someone had obviously warned the woman not to speak with any tall strangers, and as soon as Longarm iden-tified herself, damned if she didn't gather her gaggle of children together and point Longarm out to them, loudly and rather nastily informing them that they were under no circumstances to speak with him, listen to him, or accept bribes from him.

"Even candy, mama?" one smartaleck little peckerwood asked.

"If he offers you candy, Jeremy, you can take it. Then kick him in the shin and run like crazy."

The rotten little pukes had gotten quite a laugh out of that one. Dammit.

Longarm's mood was at something less than his best when he turned and headed back toward the center of town.

He hadn't minded the hike out to the Meyers farm on the north edge of Addington, but he wasn't so crazy about the long and dusty walk back.

He was, he thought, about halfway there when he heard a shy, female voice call out to him. "Yoo hoo. Mister deputy man."

The voice came from the shaded porch of an old but once rather fine house. Once-white paint was dull and peeling now, but the lines of the place were good—upright and severe but in nice proportion. The porch roof protected the ground floor from the heat of the day, and a trio of hugely magnificent oaks spread their protection to the upper floor. A vine-bearing trellis lent privacy to most of the porch, and it was from behind the leafy screen of a flowering vine—Longarm had no idea in hell what variety the white flowers were but they were pretty and smelled kinda nice—that the voice called out to him.

"Yes'm?"

"Do you have a minute?"

"Yes, of course." He didn't know who it was. But the sound being that of a voice, not a shot, why not respond to the offer?

He was a mite surprised when he mounted the porch stairs and could see behind the vines to discover that the lady was the thin young woman who'd waited on him in the ice cream parlor the day before. It took him a second or two to bring her name back to mind.

"Miss Clarice," he said as he removed his Stetson and swept it low, bowing slightly as he did so.

"You are very mannerly," she said. And then rather impishly added, "For a Northerner."

"Is that what I am?"

"Isn't it?"

He smiled. But did not otherwise answer.

"Warm today, isn't it?" she suggested.

"Yes."

"I saw you go by earlier. It was quite a while ago."

"I suppose it was at that."

"You must be thirsty."

"A little."

"Would you care for some lemonade?"

"That sounds right nice, ma'am." He remembered the silliness he'd encouraged yesterday, playing at having a limp wrist, and wondered if she would have offered something with more authority if he hadn't done that.

"Please sit and join me." She already had a pitcher of cool lemonade on a small table beside her. And an extra tumbler as well. He began to wonder if she'd been sitting here waiting for a chance to speak to him. Well, information can come from the strangest sources. And any of it was welcome so far as he was concerned.

"It would be my pleasure, ma'am."

"You may call me Clarice if you like."

"My name is Long."

"Yes, so I heard."

"My friends call me Longarm."

"Then I hope I shall be so privileged."

Stuffy. But then this was a girl from what was left of the Old South. Perhaps such formality was only to be expected in certain quarters here.

"Please do. And may I call you Clarice?"

"Yes, of course." She poured lemonade for him and refilled her own glass.

They sipped in silence for a few minutes, Longarm not sure what it was she wanted to bring up and Clarice apparently was in no hurry to get to it. Or else unsure how to go about broaching her topic, which he concluded was the more likely of the two considering that she seemed so solemn and serious of expression.

While he waited he looked at her more closely than he had bothered at the ice cream parlor the day before.

She was a tall girl and very thin. Yesterday she had been wearing a uniform of sorts, but today she was all ruffles and flounces, her dress of a style that seemed outmoded to his untrained eye but which fitted her nicely. The ivory-colored cloth was cut low at the neck, exposing the small swells of undersized breasts and a slim, rather patrician neck and hollowed collarbones.

Yesterday her hair had been pulled back into a severe bun. Today it was a mass of loose curls the color of wild honey. She wore an ivory ribbon in her hair and another at her throat, with a cameo suspended there.

She really would have been pretty had it not been for the tragedy of the wart that rode the side of her nose with all the malicious ugliness of a leech. He couldn't help wondering why she did not have the blemish removed. It was a simple enough procedure, safe and inexpensive. Not that it was any of his business what she did. But he couldn't help wondering nonetheless.

"May I ask you something, Dep . . ." She paused, smiled. "Longarm?"

"Anything you wish."

"Do you like little boys?"

"Some better'n others," he said. The thought of the Meyers kids came to mind when she asked it. That particular bunch he could do without.

"Yesterday you spoke with the little Carlton boy."

"I did?"

"At the park. You played with him on the teeter-totter."

He shrugged. What a strange thing for people to be talking about. Hell, he'd forgotten it himself. Now it turned out that this young woman knew all about it. Weird.

"You should understand that the people here do not . . . accept things that are beyond the norm."

"What's your point?" he asked.

"I understand that you . . . well, I understand. That is all I meant to say on the subject. That and that . . . you should watch yourself. If anything were to happen . . . the people here would not take it at all well. Not at all."

What in tarnation was she . . . ? Then it dawned on him. Yesterday he'd played like he was something that he wasn't. And then just a little while later he'd been seen at that damn teeter-totter. And now . . .

Shit, if folks hereabouts got to thinking he was the sort of miserable SOB who'd prey on small children, there wouldn't be manpower enough in the whole damn state to keep the straitlaced farts in the area from hanging him from a tall, tall tree. Deserve it or not, it could happen.

Just went to show that a fellow could outsmart himself if he wasn't careful. It was something he likely should keep in mind.

"And I was thinking," Clarice was pressing on, "that, well, the truth is that I don't know of anyone with the same, um, inclinations. Not anywhere in the county, actually. And I would know. So I am afraid that as long as you are here, you will just have to control yourself."

He wasn't real sure, but he kinda thought he could feel some heat building in his cheeks. Just what the hell did she think . . . never mind, he already *knew* what she thought. And it wasn't very flattering. Nor accurate for that matter. But it was without question his own stupid fault. Lordy!

"I do have a, well, an alternative of sorts. If you would like to consider it."

"Pardon?"

"You are a handsome man, Longarm."

"Thank you. You're a very pretty woman." That was real close to being true.

"We both know better. But we also know that to someone of your, uh, impulses, that does not matter in any event."

"Clarice, I think there is something I should tell you before you go any further."

"No, please. Let me finish. I've . . . the truth is, Longarm, I have spent most of the entire night past in deep contemplation about this. And I want to propose an . . . experiment, I suppose you might call it."

"Yes?"

"I think, that is to say there really is nothing to stop, I mean to tell you that . . ." She stopped and seemed quite unable to go on.

Longarm waited patiently for her to get herself together. For some reason that he could not begin to fathom, Clarice—he had no idea what her last name was and did not think this would be a good time to ask—seemed quite flustered. She was breathing heavily and was flushed of a sudden, her normally fair complexion mottled and splotched with varying shades of red and purple.

"I would like to offer myself as a substitute, Longarm. It would be, like I said, an experiment. For both of us. If you, um, see what I mean."

"I'm not real sure that I do. I mean, it kinda sounds like . . ."

"There isn't anything that a boy can do for you that I can't. Really. And . . . won't you at least *try*? What harm could there possibly be in trying? Just once. To, well, to see how it goes. So to speak."

She was blushing right furiously at this point and looking everywhere, anywhere except at him. Her hands were knotted in her lap, clenching and unclenching, rending and tearing at one another. It was a wonder she didn't hurt herself.

"Are you really saying . . . ?"

"I am saying . . . I am saying I would like you to come upstairs with me. To . . . to my bedroom. To my bed. That is,

103

uh, that is exactly what I am saying.''

"Oh, my.''

How the hell did he get himself into these things? He hadn't really meant anything by that foolishness yesterday. And now this. Shee-double-it.

"Please,'' she asked in a barely audible whisper.

She stood and without looking back started toward the front door of the once-fine house.

Chapter 26

For such an eager little thing she didn't seem all that eager.

That is, it was plain that she wanted to. But she sure as hell was shy and awkward about the whole thing once she got it started.

She took him upstairs to a pink and fluffy bedroom that smelled of rose water and a dozen other delicate scents and that looked like no male had ever seen it nor was ever intended to.

Once there she kept her back to him, as if in a display of modesty, yet she wasted no time shucking out of her clothes. With a slick, quick display of speed she got herself naked. Very nicely naked at that.

The damned wart wasn't at all noticeable once her dress was tossed onto a nearby chair.

She had a lovely body, slim and in perfect proportion. Her breasts were small but set above such a tiny waist that anything more would have seemed gross and unattractive. Her nipples were wee, proud buds of a soft and lovely pink, and her pubic hair was scant and pale atop a plump and lovely little mound.

Her skin—the soft texture of fine velveteen—was flawless, not marred by so much as a freckle much less any warts or pimples.

Had she been formed of marble she would have been exhibited in the finest of museums.

As it was, she was lovely, and Longarm's response was immediate and hearty, his erection shoving insistently at the fly of his trousers.

"Do I disgust you?" she asked, slowly turning fully around. Her back was as perfectly formed as her breasts, the soft musculature well defined and completely visible beneath her flawless skin. Her hips swelled nicely, the cheeks of her ass were small, softly curved, and apple shaped. Longarm thought it might be rather nice to take a bite out of them. Or, um, something to that effect.

"You're beautiful," he assured her. And he meant it. The imperfection on her face was completely forgotten now. He probably could not have seen it now if he'd looked for it.

Clarice smiled. And shyly came to him.

He bent, and she lifted her lips to his. The taste of her mouth was sweet and clean. Her lips were so soft and warm they seemed to have no substance, yet the tip of her tongue was saucy and tantalizing. In a way she seemed almost virginal to him, but it was clear that she was a girl who knew how to get the most out of—and give the most back with—her kisses.

Her flesh was cool and incredibly smooth, and he ran his hands lightly over her back and down to her waist, cupped the left cheek of her butt in one hand and felt the small of her back with the other.

He slid one hand in between their bodies and was shocked to discover that the hand at her back and the one touching her belly were but a few scant inches apart. She was so slim it seemed barely possible that a woman's fully grown-up body could be complete in so small a space.

Her mouth moved gently on his, and her tongue flickered and lightly darted, fencing and playing with his as he savored the taste of her kiss.

She pulled back from him a fraction of an inch but remained so close that he could feel the featherlight touch of her moving lips on his when she whispered, "May I?"

He nodded, neither knowing nor caring what it was she wanted to do, and after a moment he could feel Clarice's fingers gently tugging, pulling, slipping buttons, and undoing buckles. He let her undress him.

"Oh, my!" She stared with . . . what? amazement? surprise? perhaps a touch of fear? . . . at the strong, pulsing shaft of engorged manflesh that her activity disclosed. "I didn't . . . I mean I never . . ."

She dropped to her knees in front of him and spent long moments just looking at him before finally reaching up to gently very gently touch and caress him.

Then, every bit as gently, she leaned closer. She breathed in deeply and he almost would have sworn that she was taking in his scent. Odd, he thought. Damned odd. But sweet.

And then once more the pink tip of her tongue crept out and, very lightly, she tasted him. Kissed the underside of the red and shiny head. His pecker jerked in response to the touch, and Clarice jumped back away from him as if startled.

When she realized that his pole was not actually chasing her—or whatever it was she'd thought it was doing—she laughed, the sound of it light and happy, and leaned forward again, this time to repeat the experiment, but deliberately, obviously delighting in her ability to provoke such a reaction.

"Havin' fun?" he asked.

"As a matter of fact I am, yes." She grinned up at him and then flicked her tongue over the small slit in the end of his prick, clapping her hands with joy at his bouncing, jumping reaction to the touch. "Are they all like this?" she asked.

"Damn if I'd know. This here's the only one o' the things I've ever had."

She gave him an odd look, and he was reminded that she thought he had considerably more experience in that regard than was the case. Still, this didn't seem exactly the right moment to be giving explanations. Another time maybe. Not now.

Clarice bent forward again, this time taking the head delicately into her mouth. He was engulfed with a damp, sweet warmth. And then with a sharp pain.

107

"No teeth, please," he told her.

"Oops. Sorry."

Damn girl didn't mind giving head. But she acted like it was something she'd never ever done before.

For that matter, she was treating his cock like she'd never seen one before and yet she was bold as brass when it came to inviting him into her bed.

Odd girl, Clarice. But lovely. And plenty of pleasure to be with.

He let her examine, touch and taste for a while, then took her by the hands and guided her gently onto her feet.

He bent, slipped one strong arm behind her back and the other at her knees and picked her up. She weighed next to nothing.

"Shall we?" He inclined his head in the direction of the big bed with its canopy of pink and white ruffles.

"Yes. Please."

He carried her to the bed and lowered her onto it with a long, deep kiss.

She felt like little more than a wraith in his arms. A wisp. So slight she seemed hardly to exist, yet so warm and soft and accommodating.

Her arms wrapped close about his neck, and her kisses were slow and good.

After a bit, almost as an afterthought, he raised himself over her, allowing his legs to intrude between her knees so that she was open to him.

He kissed her breasts and her belly and felt the warm fluids at her crotch that told him she was ready.

She began to moan and pulse her hips in response to his touching, and he shifted position so that he was poised at the opening to her slim body.

Gently he lowered himself onto her. Into her. There was a moment of resistance. And then with a rush he plunged the rest of the way inside Clarice.

She gasped and clutched him in a sudden, convulsive spasm that as quickly subsided, and after that it was fine.

He stroked deep into her, and she responded eagerly and with growing pleasure, her breathing quickening and soon becoming ragged as her climax built and built and soon exploded well in advance of his own.

Finally, when both of them were spent, Longarm lay atop her, careful to take most of his weight on his knees and elbows while she held him in the embrace of arms and legs alike.

"How nice," she whispered. "Do you know something?"

"Mm."

"I really like having sex with a man. I don't care what Aunt Edith says. It's even better with a man than with a girl." With that she closed her eyes and, with a sigh of contentment, seemed to drift away into a light sleep.

Longarm, on the other hand, was wide awake. He was much too old and experienced to be shocked by anything any-damn-body might say or do.

But damned if Clarice hadn't come mighty close to it.

Chapter 27

Longarm lounged atop the big bed with his arms behind his head, his legs crossed at the ankles and a sense of deep contentment so complete, his belly and balls felt emptied, drained.

Clarice did not want him to smoke in her bed—something about the smell of it lingering, and she didn't want anyone to know about her guest—but he didn't mind that. Not considering the alternative she suggested.

Clarice, it turned out, was entirely content to spend endless time happily licking and sucking on a nipple. Something to do with bottle deprivation was a child, no doubt. And while her normal target apparently was the nipple attached to a nicely rounded female breast she did not at all mind switching to a harder and flatter surface. And from Longarm's perspective, well, he hadn't known just how completely sensitive a man's nipples could be when exposed to such exhaustive a regimen as that provided by the young Miss Clarice. He could feel the pleasure tingling all the way into his groin, and if the girl didn't watch herself she was going to get something started. Him, for instance.

Not that he thought she would mind. Getting started, along with finishing it, was an activity she seemed to take to almighty well now that she'd tried it.

"Tell me something," he said.

"Mm?"

"Were you really a virgin?"

She giggled. "For the, what? tenth time? yes. Technically speaking. I mean, I've had sex for almost as long as I can remember. Since I was a girl. But never with a man before." She laughed. "It felt nice."

"You're really . . . ?"

"Lesbian is the word you are looking for, I think. The same as you but the female version of it. And, yes, I am one. At least, I always thought that I was. Now I'm not so sure. A good little lesbian is supposed to hate the mere thought of being with a man. But once I got to thinking about you, well, I have to admit that I found the idea exciting. That was just in theory. In actual practice," she rolled her eyes and grinned, "it really was a lot of fun."

She abandoned his left nipple and sat upright beside him. "You didn't seem to have any trouble getting interested in me either."

This was a good time to correct her past misimpressions. On the other hand, why destroy a perfectly good delusion? If the girl wanted to think she'd accomplished a first, and maybe saved some innocent kid in the bargain, why the hell not? "Not only got interested," he said, "I think I could be again."

"Really?" The thought did not appear to make her cringe.

"Throw a lip-lock on that dead soldier down there and see what happens," he suggested.

Clarice laughed. And bent her head to his middle, enveloping him in the wet heat of her mouth.

Nope, he had no trouble at all rising to the occasion.

Half an hour or so later he stretched, utterly worn out now but not minding that in the least, and reached for a cheroot. Barely in time he remembered Clarice's prohibition against smoking, and put the cigar back into a pocket. "Damn shame you don't live here alone," he complained, seriously wanting the taste of a good smoke now in the aftermath of such a good blow job.

"It's lucky for me I have a place to live at all. This isn't

111

my home, actually. I'm just a poor relation.''

"Oh?''

"This is my Aunt Edith's house. You remember her, I'm sure.''

"I do?''

"She owns the ice cream parlor. You saw her yesterday at the store.''

"The older woman with the hair like slicked-back steel wool?''

"If she ever heard you say that she'd probably grab a knife and try to cut your balls off. She just might be able to manage it, too. But, yes, that's her.''

"She isn't . . . ?''

"A lesbian too? Of course she is. All of us girls are.''

"All of . . . ?''

"Me, my cousin Barb . . . she's my other aunt's daughter though I don't' know how my aunt Doris ever had a baby, hating men just as badly as Edith does . . . and my other cousin Louise. Louise is my mother's brother's daughter. My mom and her brother are all dead, of course. Only Doris is left now. And Herbert. But he doesn't count.''

"No?''

"No. We never talk about Herbert. He's the black sheep of the family.''

"Let me get this straight. Doris and all the rest of you girls are lesbians, and most of the family is dead, but you don't talk about Herbert because he did something the rest of you are ashamed of. Is that right?''

"Pretty much so, yes.'' She bent down and began licking a convenient nipple again but this time he was just too far gone to get much out of it. Although it did feel rather good, come to think of it.

"What the hell did Herbert do to deserve that?'' he asked.

"Really, Longarm dear, we don't like to talk about it. Does this feel good?''

"Better'n I woulda thought possible at this point.''

"What about this?''

112

"That's even better."

"And . . . this?"

"Oh, jeez. You better quit that or else."

"Or else what?" There was a glimmer of impishly evil glee in her eyes when she asked that question.

"Well, uh . . ."

"And what about *this*?"

"I'll be damned."

"That may be true, dear. But not until I've had my fun again. Now hold still . . . no, lift your leg just a little so I can wriggle under . . . yes, like that . . . a little more, please . . . hold still. *Oh*!"

She began to laugh with unabashed delight.

And Longarm, incredibly enough, began to respond, the dead returning slowly but inexorably to life one more time.

He closed his eyes and let the girl have her way.

Chapter 28

"Where the hell have you been?"

"Layin' down on the job," Longarm answered. Which of course was considerably more true than Amos was ever likely to know.

"Well you went and missed the excitement."

"Oh?"

"Our killer has been at it again. Or killers, as in more than one of them, which is more likely."

"Who this time?"

"The town clerk."

"James Deel?"

"I'll be damned," Amos said. "For someone the towns-people won't talk to, you seem to be pretty well-informed. Yeah, the man was Jim Deel. You know him, I take it?"

Longarm shook his head. "No, but that informant I told you about mentioned Deel as a possible suspect."

"I think we can prob'ly strike him off the short list of sus-pects," the scrawny Ranger drawled.

"How was he killed?"

"Same old deal. Somebody came a-tapping at his door. He opened it and, boom. Took one square in the face at a range so close the powder burn made him look like a raccoon."

"Efficient," Longarm said.

114

"Our boy, or boys, are good at what they do."

"What time did all this happen?"

"Morning, this time. Just about dawn."

"No witnesses, of course."

"Not unless you count the wife, and she didn't actually see anything. She was in the kitchen mixing up a batch of biscuit dough. She's in hysterics now, thinking it's all her fault. She said Deel was on his way out to the backhouse for his morning shit . . . well, that's what she meant even if it isn't quite the way she put it . . . and she's the one heard the knocking at the door and asked him to see who it was before he went out the other way. Said she had her hands all covered in flour or she would have gone and it would have been her dead instead of him."

"I'm not so sure she's right about that," Longarm said.

"Chief Bender is trying to convince her. Hell, whoever it is who wants all these people dead wants them, not their families. If she'd gone to the door . . . and my guess is that the shooter was peeking in to make sure it was likely the right party would show up ready for slaughter . . . if she'd gone I bet it would have been somebody pretending to get the wrong house. Some excuse or other. He wouldn't have shot the lady of the place anyway, I bet."

"Or would have and then come in to finish the job properly. You never know. Whatever might have happened, she's alive now and that's a good thing. Any kids involved?"

"No kids." Amos made a sour face. "I always hate it too when there's kids left without a daddy. I guess it shouldn't make any difference. Dead is dead. But I always think of it as being worse."

"Yeah." Longarm fired up a fresh cheroot—he was making up for lost time now that he was out of Clarice's house—and offered one to Amos, who declined. "You've found out an awful lot for a fella who isn't supposed to be a cop."

"Unlike you, my friend, I am a very sympathetic soul in Addington. The bereaved cousin and all that. So when I heard my dead cuz's murderer struck again, I naturally hustled over there to see what was what. The chief and I get along just fine.''

"And Sergeant Braxton?''

"His balls aren't the only things made of solid brass, you know. So is his brain. Solid from one ear clean through to the other. I don't like that man. Don't trust him. Neither does the major or I wouldn't be here. The only problem is that he has a lot of powerful friends, and there is no clear evidence to use as an excuse to get rid of the son of a bitch.''

"So much for the camaraderie of brothers in arms, an' all that dreary horseshit.''

"I feel toward Brass Braxton just about as kindly as you would to a deputy on the take. Okay?''

"I reckon that pretty well says it, all right,'' Longarm agreed.

"You gonna look into Deel's murder?''

"Damn right I am. Do you happen to know if the chief remembered yet t' warn the new widow that she oughtn't t' talk to me?''

"I don't know, but if he hasn't done it yet he soon will. That man don't like you, Longarm. Not worth a shit, he don't.''

"Reckon I better go have a word with Mrs. Deel quick if I'm ever going to then.''

Amos nodded. And told him how to find the latest victim's house.

"Thanks, Lester. See you tonight?''

"I'll drop by if I don't have anything better to do.''

Longarm touched the brim of his Stetson and strode away in the direction of the Deel residence.

Town clerk, dammit. A citizen, then the postmaster, then the county's Whig secretary, and now the Addington town clerk. It occurred to Longarm that he'd forgotten to ask Amos if the town's records had been tampered with. Or for that matter if anyone had yet thought to look into that.

If nothing had been disturbed yet, well, maybe it wouldn't be a bad idea to keep an eye on City Hall tonight. Just to see if there were any nocturnal visitors.

Chapter 29

Peter Nare hadn't had any living family, and the other murders were pretty much in the past by the time Longarm arrived on the scene. But Jim Deel must have been a popular fellow, and his death was fresh and shocking. The town was turning out in huge numbers to express their sympathies to the bereaved widow.

It was midafternoon when Longarm got to the Deel residence, and the killing had taken place just that morning. Already, though, there was a regular procession of friends, neighbors, and probably total strangers, too, marching in through a wide-open doorway with platters of sliced ham or fried chicken, huge mounds of mashed potatoes, fragrant casseroles, and tray after tray after tray of freshly baked bread, rolls, biscuits, pies, cupcakes, layer cakes, and hoecakes. Whether among the cotton fields of east Texas, the sugar bush of Vermont, or the green valleys of Oregon, the American belief is and always has been that grief is best assuaged by hiding it under an onslaught of foods. The good folks of Addington were just proving that penchant now.

Women, giggling girls, and grubby-faced little boys walked, ran, or scampered through the yard and down the side streets.

A dusty patch of yard beneath a drooping oak seemed to have been set aside as a nursery where toddlers and crawling children were deposited, and the older girl children showed signs of being more or less in charge there.

Two hams and a meat loaf arrived at the same time Longarm did, the women carrying them bustling past him on the walkway between the gate and front porch, their mission too intense to allow time for normal politeness. After all, one of their own was in pain and therefore in need of the twin reminders that the other ladies cared . . . and that life goes on regardless of loss and grief. For that too was hidden within the messages of the food platters. Weep for the dead but do not neglect to feed the living.

Longarm mounted the steps to the broad porch and removed his hat. The door was already propped open to receive the callers, so he shouldered his way in behind a plump lady carrying a pot of steaming, aromatic baked beans.

A parlor to his left held a bunch of women and elderly men, all of them gathered close around a large, red-faced and stunned-looking woman in her thirties or thereabouts. That would be the widow Deel, of course.

Ahead and to his right the dining-room table was sagging from the weight of the foods that had been piled a couple feet deep atop it—well, it looked to be that deep anyhow—and additional space had been created by someone taking a door off its hinges and laying it onto a pair of chairs turned to face inward. A similar arrangement would no doubt be prepared, if a little more carefully, to hold the coffin in the parlor once the undertaker was done with the remains of the dear departed.

At the back of the narrow hallway he could see through into the kitchen where there were so many women crammed into the place that if someone on the south end got a pain in the belly, someone on the north end would surely feel the contractions as they passed from one to the other like ripples in a small pond.

A middle-aged woman whose expression showed the compassion of a saint and the raw determination of an infantry-corps commander took Longarm by the elbow and steered him in the direction of the dining room. She was a little bit of a thing, the top of her head coming about up to his third shirt button, but that didn't slow her down. She had as good a hold of him as a kid leading a bull by a ring through its nose, and he was darn well going wherever she chose to take him.

"I know you haven't had a chance yet to speak to Jessica, I saw you come in just now, but you can't go in yet, she's with the preacher and they're praying and then he will want her to tell him what Jim's favorite hymns were and take care of all those little details for the service, and I'm sure you understand, so please be patient, have yourself something to eat and wait here until the preacher and his missus leave and then you can go in, and don't worry, I'll keep an eye out and come get you to tell you you can go in then, all right?" She smiled up at him and continued dragging him on into the dining room without ever once giving thought to whether or not he wanted to go there. She wanted him to go there, he was going there, and that was that.

Longarm looked at the little woman with no small amount of awe. Damn if she didn't seem to have conquered the need to breathe. Sure seemed to have, anyway. She'd got all that out in one seamless rush, which he would not have believed except that he'd heard it his own self and would swear to the fact in a court of law if called upon.

"Yes, ma'am." It was about the only response that was open to him.

The little woman put a plate in his hand, the china so freshly washed that it was still warm and slightly damp from rinse water incompletely dried off.

"The meats are at this end, so start here and don't be shy. There's more in the kitchen and more on the way."

"Yes, ma'am."

"And if you need anything that you can't find here"—she smiled up at him—"then you are entirely too picky and can stand to do without for right now."

Longarm smiled back at her. "Yes, ma'am."

Satisfied, the little woman turned and whisked herself away into the kitchen—who'd have thought there was room enough in there for her to squeeze in and never mind how small she was?—leaving him standing in the midst of all that food with a plate in one hand and a set of silverware in the other.

And come to think of it, he was pretty hungry. He hadn't gotten around to lunch yet today. And damn but those oven-baked beans had smelled good, and now there was all this succulent ham and other goodies laid out in front of him.

He shrugged and commenced to fill his plate.

Chapter 30

"You son of a bitch!"

Longarm looked up in time to see a fist coming his way. He took half a step back, and Chief of Police J. Michael Bender's rather impulsively thrown punch went soaring past without damaging anything more than J. Michael Bender's pride.

"Is there something you wanta . . ."

Damned if the man didn't try it again. A hard jab this time. Longarm swayed to his left.

"Careful now, I just got me some of these little meatball things an' . . ."

The chief was nothing if not persistent. He tried it a third time. Unfortunately—or not, depending on one's point of view—Longarm didn't pull his plate quite all the way aside with him this time. The police chief's forearm jostled Longarm's wrist and somehow—he was awfully sorry about that—a dinner plate nearly full of beans swimming in sticky-sweet, melted brown sugar and molasses wound up decorating the front of Bender's coat and mighty expensive-looking necktie. The meatballs bounced a few times and ended up rolling around the floor, but those beans had pretty good sticking power.

Three punches. Which Longarm considered to be something in excess of enough.

"Now look, goddammit, if you don't quit I'm apt t' get a mite angry here," Longarm said. Ducking a moment afterward underneath a looping, roundhouse right. Inexpert but intense. Real intense. It actually might have hurt if it had landed.

Bender tried a final blow.

And, as the saying goes, that one took the rag off'n the bush.

Longarm dropped the fork he was still holding onto—the plate by then was long gone, sadly shattered and underfoot by this time—and reached out.

The chief's momentum was already carrying him forward. Longarm decided there was no sense in wasting a perfectly good advantage. He tugged a bit here and pushed a speck there, and Bender found himself turned clean around and facing in the other direction.

Which happened to be toward the broad doorway leading from the dining room into the entry hall. And on toward the wide-open front door.

Not a bad idea, Longarm thought.

At the same time that he took one flailing arm by the wrist and pulled it behind the man's back, he also got a good grip on Bender's collar. And lifted, scooting the man forward on tiptoes at the same time.

Worked right nicely if he did say so himself.

Bender tippy-toed right out of the Deel dining room, through the vestibule, and outside to where there wasn't quite such a crowd.

Although by this time one could reasonably say that attention had been diverted from the widow and was now centered on a couple of the grieving guests. Like, for instance, on the two who were scuffling on the porch. But then, distractions like that do tend to add spice to a wake. Or whatever this pre-funeral gathering should be called. Longarm wasn't real sure about that.

What he was sure about was that Chief Bender was hissing and fuming and sounding like a tea kettle that was about to pop its lid.

The man was so purely frazzled and furious that he wasn't

122

coherent. He was past any ability to form individual words and seemed to be settling for making all possible sounds, all at one and the same time.

Longarm clucked in sympathy.

And propelled the man right on across the porch and over the railing.

Turned him plumb upside down in the process. And then gave him a little shove while he was airborne.

The chief of police of Addington, Texas, landed head first in Jessica Deel's lilacs.

About the only thing that could have made it any better—in Longarm's admittedly prejudiced opinion—would have been if Mrs. Deel went in for native cacti instead of flowery things.

But then, after all, a fellow can't have everything in life. Quite.

Bender landed with a yelp and a great wallowing and thrashing, hung suspended there for a few moments, and then with a crackling and crashing of greenery, sank near out of sight into a bed of dying hollyhocks.

It was, Longarm thought, entertainment of the first water.

J. Michael Bender, on the other hand, did not seem amused.

The man came sputtering and roaring out of the shrubbery—upright, this time—and looked for half a moment like he was going to make the ultimate mistake and grab for his revolver.

Longarm wasn't one to find fun in playing with guns. Particularly when they were wielded by irrational assholes. Which Bender was acting to a fare-thee-well.

Bender's hand had a chance to get just the least bit twitchy, and the next thing he knew, he was looking into the huge, gaping muzzle—only forty-five hundredths of an inch across by careful measure, but at least a yard wide when seen from Bender's unique angle of view—of Longarm's Colt.

The chief dropped any notions about appealing to Sam Colt for equality in action and went more than a little pale.

"You . . . you . . . I will get you for this, Long. Either get out of my town and out of my jurisdiction or so help me, I'll . . . I'll . . .''

"If you got a complaint, Chief, you best file it with my boss. I'll give one o' your people the address t' make sure you get it right. But don't make the mistake o' trying me, mister. I won't take but so much. You hear me? Any more stupidity like this an' I'll put you in irons for assault on a federal officer. Guaranteed. What's more, I'll make it stick. There's federal judges that owe me some favors, an' for you I'd call my markers in.''

That was a lie but what the hell, Bender didn't know it.

"An' don't you forget, Chief. Your jurisdiction, such as it is, stops at the city limits. There ain't no place in this whole country that's outa mine. You get my meaning? Now get the hell outa here before you go an' do something you can't call back after.''

Longarm waited until the chief departed, leaving his dignity behind, then followed.

He didn't think this would work out to be a real good time now to try and interview the widow Deel.

Those sure as hell had been good beans, though.

Chapter 31

"Must talk. Be in your room 7:30." Longarm looked at the sloppy scrawl on the note the desk clerk had handed him. He did not recognize the handwriting but figured it pretty much had to be Amos who wanted to meet.

That being the case he first checked his Ingersoll to make sure of the time, then went down the block to find a saloon where he could lay in a bottle of corn whiskey. He had a little rye left in his bag, but why waste the good stuff on a man who preferred spiked dishwater to the nectar of Maryland's finest distillers?

Well before the appointed hour—he didn't need any supper thanks to the late and huge lunch he'd had at the Deel house—Longarm was in his hotel room.

Promptly at 7:30 there was a soft tap-tap-tap on the hotel room door.

"Amos?"

The tapping sounded again.

Longarm swung the door open. And without much in the way of either warning or preamble found his tongue being sucked out of his mouth. The widow Jane Webster Sproul had arrived.

"I'm so glad you got my message," she said when she paused for breath. Then she grabbed him again and put a lip-lock on so hard, he was afraid she would bruise her tonsils on his front teeth. The woman was nothing if not energetic.

"Whoa, Janie, what's this all about?"

She grinned at him. And began flinging clothes toward the four corners of the room. "This, sweetie. I just couldn't stand being without you. Not for another minute."

Longarm didn't have the heart to tell her that he was already too worn out from his morning of playing with Clarice to possibly be able to get it up again. Maybe not for days to come, judging from the way he felt right now.

And in truth he couldn't much claim to being interested in Jane's floppy, flabby figure. Not after being with a slim and vibrant little slip of a thing like Clarice. The differences between the two were just too startling to ignore.

Besides, dammit, he was tired. He didn't *want* to be the object, no matter how affectionately, of some crazy woman's fantasies.

And besides that . . .

Too late. Janie was naked by then—and if he ever wanted an enemy for life he was sure he knew how to get one: just let a woman, any woman, get naked and offer herself to him, then reject the offer; that would do the job all right—and she was on her knees, busily unfastening the buttons at his fly.

Longarm smothered a sigh and let the fool woman go ahead with what she was doing. She would find out for herself soon enough that she was pursuing a lost cause. He just plain didn't have anything left down there to give her.

"Oh. Beautiful. This is just so pretty, sweetie. So nice."

She had his shorts down around his ankles now, leaving only a middling growth of public hair in place to defend his modesty.

"If I could paint, honey, I'd do a drawing of this thing," she cooed. "Better yet I wish I could sculpt." She laughed. "That way I'd have a little something to fall back on whenever you weren't around."

He could feel her breath on his skin. Very sensitive down

there at the moment. Worn-out but sensitive nonetheless, oh yes it was.

He could feel her breath and then he could feel her lips and next her tongue. Damn, but the woman's mouth was warm. It felt almost hot around him. And nicely wet. It was . . . soothing. Pleasant. He was too tired to say it excited him exactly. But it felt mighty nice regardless.

She played with his balls while she sucked and gobbled at him for a spell, then with a wink turned herself around and kind of slithered underneath his crotch, forcing her head between his legs so that she could reach his asshole with her tongue. Janie Sproul was no shrinking violet, uh-uh. She gave him a rimming and a bit of a reaming and came up grinning at herself because by the time she was done doing that, he had a hard-on that a cat couldn't have scratched. Damn thing was like polished marble. Hell, the head was engorged so full of blood that the skin was shiny.

Longarm was impressed. Also amazed.

"Are you gonna put that pretty thing in me, honey? Or what?"

"Reckon I can handle that if you insist, ma'am," he said in an exaggerated drawl.

Janie laughed. And grabbed him by the pecker to lead him the few steps across the room to the bed.

The woman, he thought, was not exactly shy, was she?

Chapter 32

He was drowsing, half-asleep, when a light tapping on the room door wakened him. He sat upright with the thought that he'd already done this. He remembered it for certain sure. Except it wasn't an exact repeat of a previous experience, couldn't be, because this time Janie Sproul was occupying the right-hand two thirds of the rumpled and sweaty bed and was snoring just a little. A delicate and ladylike creature. Uh-huh.

Longarm shook his head, bit a yawn back behind chattering teeth and stood upright. Groggy and disoriented though he was, he plucked the Colt from its holster draped over the bedpost, and carried the revolver with him as he stumbled his way to the door.

"Who is it and do you have an awful good reason t' be there?"

"It's me. Amos."

"Oh, Lester. Right."

"Let me in."

"That wouldn't be, uh, convenient right now."

"Then meet me downstairs in the lobby. Ten minutes?"

"That sounds all right, Lester." He glanced back toward the bed where Janie was awake and listening. He hoped she hadn't heard "Lester Colton" announce himself as someone named Amos. Particularly not after Longarm had mistaken her

128

knock for the arrival of someone named Amos just a few hours earlier. ''Ten minutes.'' He waited until he heard footsteps receding down the corridor, then started gathering up the clothes that were scattered hither and yon throughout the room, tossing the female items toward the bed and dragging on his own things as he came to them.

''Something important?'' Janie asked.

''A friend wants t' buy me a drink.''

''You'd leave my bed for that?''

''T' begin with, it ain't your bed, it's mine. Secondly, in my line o' work you never know when or where you might find out something worth knowing. If somebody wants t' have a talk, then I reckon I'd best set down and keep my ears open. You know?''

''No, but I'll take your word for it.''

''Thank you.''

Janie began getting herself dressed. He was glad to see that. He'd been quite frankly worried that she might want to stay the night. He really was not up to that tonight. What he wanted now, badly, was about eighteen uninterrupted hours of sleep. That and a breakfast they'd have to serve in a bushel basket. If he could just manage those two things, then maybe he could face the world again.

He finished dressing first—what is it about women that makes it impossible for them to pull a pair of bloomers over their asses in less than seven minutes by an actual, timed clock?—and lighted a cheroot. Janie took it from him, and he lighted another for himself.

''Tell me, sweetie,'' she said.

''Hmm?'' He wasn't entirely sure he was awake. It felt more like he was pretending to be while in reality he was sort of viewing things from somewhere high and to the right of his corporeal self.

''Have you gotten any information ·about where to find Buddy?''

''Who?''

"My first husband. The one who's been murdering all these people. Remember?"

"Oh. Right." He yawned. He didn't know if he should tell her that she was wrong about Buddy Matthews or just let her enjoy her own delusions for the time being.

"I heard he was seen over in Avondale," Janie said.

"Do tell."

"That doesn't mean a thing to you, does it?"

"Never heard of the place," he admitted.

"It's a community of mostly Hungarians southwest of here about five miles. They raise chickens, most of them. They sell eggs as far away as New Orleans. And buy more water glass to store their eggs in than all the rest of Texas put together. How's that for a fascinating point of interest?"

"Fascinates me, all right."

"Are you going to arrest him?"

"Not without proof that he's committed a crime," Longarm said.

"I told you, sweetie, he's the one killing all these men. Every one of them was a member of that shivaree party that kept Buddy out of my pants on our wedding night. He hasn't forgotten. Believe me, Longarm, I know him."

"Janie, you thought you knew him when you married him. You was proved wrong that time. What makes you think you know him now when you haven't seen him in something like a hunnerd damn years?"

"I know what I'm telling you is true, Longarm. I swear to you it is."

"Look, Janie, I know you mean well. I know you believe what you've told me. But all the evidence points t' this string o' killings being political. Starting with a bunch o' silly sons o' bitches who think they can secede from the Union all by themselves when the whole of the Confederacy couldn't manage to accomplish that just a little while back. Now I hate t' tell you this, but I think you've made a mistake about your former husband an' his capacity for vengeance."

"You can't be serious! Surely, honey, you aren't as blind

as all these other idiots around here.''

"I'm sorry, Janie. Really I am. But what I just told you is the truth as I see it.''

"I thought you were different, Longarm. I thought you would listen to me.''

"I have listened, Janie. And I've given your ideas considerable thought. Now what I got t' do is find out who really shot an' killed Postmaster Colton, never mind opinion or prejudice or whatever.''

"Then go down to Avondale and look for him there, Longarm. You'll find your murderer in Avondale. Unless he's come back here to kill again.''

Longarm didn't feel up to arguing with her any more. He said, "Stay here long enough t' finish your smoke, Janie. Then it should be safe enough for you t' come downstairs.''

She gave him a sad smile and shook her head. "Don't you realize that everyone in this place already knows what room I'm visiting? You just don't understand us here, do you?''

"Maybe not, Janie. Maybe I don't at that.'' He tugged his Stetson on, bent to give her a chaste kiss on the cheek, and got the hell out of there. Amos—Lester Colton these days— was waiting in the lobby downstairs.

Chapter 33

"Having fun, Longarm?"

"Not really. It's beginning to feel like work."

"If you're looking for sympathy . . ."

Longarm grinned and offered his friend a cheroot, which Amos declined.

"Anybody I know?" Amos asked.

"That's always possible, ain't it?"

"You're just a regular little old fount of information this evening. Feeling kinda smug after this afternoon, huh?"

"This afternoon?"

"You know. The chief of police? Last I heard, him and the magistrate were talking about could they make an assault charge stick."

"Talking about could they make sure all the witnesses would stick to the party line in other words."

"I will admit that one hears two widely varying accounts about what happened," Amos said. "But I'll tell you what I think."

"What's that?"

"You should have hit the son of a bitch."

"Come again?"

"You should have punched him, Longarm. Kicked him. Beaten the shit out of him. Any one of those would have been fine. I mean, a man can stand being beat up. I never heard of anybody, you or me included, who isn't ever going to come up against somebody else who's stronger or quicker or just plain luckier on a given day. But what you did to him, Longarm, picking him up and dumping him into a rosebush . . .''

"It was only a lilac," Longarm protested. "No thorns."

"The man is skinned up pretty good."

Longarm shrugged.

"Okay, lilac, fine. The point is, his pride could have taken being beaten by you. But what you did, treating him like he was some sorry-ass kid that you didn't even have to bother whipping, that cut deep. Bone deep. Bender won't ever forgive or forget, I can tell you that much."

"T' tell you the truth, I don't much give a shit. All I want out of Addington is *out* of Addington. You know?"

"With your murderer."

"Well, yeah, with a murderer. That's what I come here t' do."

"At least in that, you have an ally you might not have counted on. Sergeant Braxton is foursquare in your corner on letting you get your man quick as possible and then get the hell out of here. Brass seems to be about the only one around who recognizes that Norm Colton's killing should be handled as a separate matter so you federals can be satisfied and the local affairs can take place without any outsiders looking on."

"If I were planning what those boys are, I think I'd follow good advice when I heard it," Longarm said.

"You, uh, wouldn't ignore a threat to the Constitution of the United States, would you?"

"Of course not. But I got to tell you that I think it would take an awful lot more than a bunch of east-Texas assholes like these Texas Firsters to represent any kind of a threat. So until or unless I see good reason t' change my mind about that, all I'm looking at here is the death of one federal employee. Any other killings the same party or parties may've done are strictly the affair of the local law, far as I can see it."

133

"I'll make sure Braxton understands that. Could be he'll convince Bender to cooperate with you instead of raising his hackles every time you come into view."

"I'd appreciate that, Lester."

"All right then. Oh, and by the way. This afternoon while you were off dancing with the police chief, I did some asking around. It seems there is some doubt about whether all the town records are intact."

"Oh?"

"And guess what sort of records they think are missing?"

Longarm waited. Hell, Amos didn't want an answer anyway. Not really.

"I heard someone at City Hall say they think the poll records and voter-registration books are missing."

"Mm, now imagine that. The Whig party secretary dead and now the town clerk. Records missing from both. This is beginning to look kinda interesting."

"Sure does give somebody room to make a fresh start, doesn't it?" Amos said.

"All I got t' say is that it's a damn good thing everybody in politics is honest, because a situation like this could give an unscrupulous person opportunity to rewrite history just about any way he wants it."

"Like excluding names off the registration lists if those people are likely to vote the wrong candidate."

"Yep, it's just a damn good thing nobody around here would stoop so low as t' do a thing like that. You thirsty, Lester?"

"I could stand a drink."

The two men stood and turned to leave the lobby. Their attention was caught, though, by a breathless messenger running in to ask the hotel clerk if he'd seen the night patrolman.

"Not for half an hour or so—why?"

"Because there's been another killing, that's why," the young man puffed. "The worst yet. It's the police chief himself that's been shot this time."

The distraught fellow bent over for a moment to gulp for

134

breath, then turned and dashed back out into the night.

"Aw, shit," Longarm mumbled. He shook his head. "Reckon we better put that drink off till later, Mr. Colton."

"Yes, I expect we should at that."

Chapter 34

Longarm and "Lester Colton" made the steep climb to the top floor of City Hall in record time. They found the expected scene of confusion there with virtually every cop on the force—there weren't really all that many, one night man, two day officers and a part-time relief officer who worked weekends and the occasional day off for the others—getting in each other's way along with Ranger Sergeant George Braxton and a handful of civilians who no doubt worked for, or anyway drew pay from, the town.

In his role as an interested spectator Amos couldn't say much, and he tried to fade into the woodwork as much as possible while Longarm stepped into the middle of things.

At that middle was the focus of all the fuss and feathers, namely the very dead body of Police Chief J. Michael Bender. The man had changed to fresh clothing since Longarm last saw him—something without brush scrapes and grass stains—and was dotted here and there with a salve to heal the scratches he'd gotten from Mrs. Deel's lilacs.

Not that he need have bothered.

There was a dark-purple depression in the center of his forehead. The dime-sized hole was surrounded by a black ring where burning gunpowder had scorched the skin.

Apart from that little flaw, though, Bender looked pretty

good. His hair was not even mussed. He was still at his desk, seated in his chair almost normally, though slumped back into a more relaxed posture than he had allowed himself in life.

There wasn't any great secret about the way the man died. He'd been sitting peacefully at his desk, expecting no difficulties, and then he was shot at virtually point-blank range.

The dead man's eyes were open, which Longarm always found a mite disconcerting. Since no one else seemed inclined to do it, Longarm went around behind the desk and pushed his eyes shut. They stayed closed without having to be weighted or sewn, which Longarm considered something of a small blessing. He hated it when you couldn't make the eyes remain closed.

Brass Braxton looked at Longarm, opened his mouth as if to protest, and then thought better of it.

Which Longarm thought damned odd. The sergeant was not a shy fellow and would almost certainly want to take over this investigation himself.

Something else occurred to Longarm, though, that was of more immediate interest than thinking about the actions and reactions of a stray Ranger sergeant. When he'd touched Bender the man had felt downright warm. He put his fingertips on Bender's throat and confirmed that fleeting impression. The body had barely begun to cool.

"Did anybody hear the shot?" he asked of no one in particular.

Since no one volunteered an answer, he selected the uniformed cop whom he recognized as the regular night officer and repeated the question to him.

"No, sir. Not that we know about."

"Any idea as to time of death then?"

"Yes, sir, we pretty much know when it has to've been."

"Care to explain that, officer?"

"Yes, sir. The chief's habit is . . . was, that is . . . to come in every night at ten. Never failed to do that, sir, not as long as I've been on the payroll. I never knew him to be late and he wasn't often more than five or ten minutes early. He always checked the incident log"—the young officer pointed to a large leather ledger book that lay on a counter at the side of the room—"and had a word with the night duty officer before he'd go home and go to bed. Every night including weekends he did that."

"And tonight?"

"The night officers know his routine, of course. We always come up between ten and ten-fifteen. Tonight I got here about ten or eleven minutes past the hour. That's when I found the chief, just like you see him now."

"So he was killed between 9:50 and, say, 10:12," Longarm said.

"Yes, sir. And by somebody he knew, of course, which I guess you can see for yourself. I mean, he was sitting down at his desk. He wasn't alarmed, wasn't worried about nothing. Whoever killed him just walked right over to him and opened up right in his face."

"Uh-huh, I . . . Sergeant, what's that you have there?"

Braxton broke into a half-trot for the door, then realized his error and stopped, turning and trying to look casual and unconcerned.

He was somewhat too late for that, however.

The man was caught red-handed—and red-faced too.

At least he did have the good grace to blush about it.

He was standing there holding a pair of ledger books, neither of these quite so fancy as the official police log book. One was a large, canvas-bound volume of the sort often found in public agencies, the other a smaller paperbound book.

"May I see what you were about to walk out with?" Longarm asked in a deceptively pleasant tone of voice.

He held his hand out and started across the room.

Brass Braxton looked once again like he would much rather run than stand still.

Chapter 35

"My oh my, will you just lookee here," Longarm muttered happily. "Now this one I'd say looks t' be the Whig-party minute book that was taken from Peter Nare's place t'other night. You ask why I'd suspect that?" he said, although no one in the room had asked any such thing or for that matter made the first bit of noise. "I kinda suspect it because it says right here on the first page that that's what it is, an' it's signed there by P. Nare. That's the first one." He set it aside, dropping it onto the corner of Bender's desk. "An' this other one here," he opened the larger more substantial volume, "this here one claims t' be an official record of voter registration for the county of . . ." He looked up at the Ranger sergeant. "Damn good police work for you to've spotted these missing pieces o' evidence, Sergeant. I'm sure your captain will be right proud o' you when this is reported. Yes sir, real good police work here."

Braxton squirmed as if his shirt collar was entirely too tight. Pity about that, Longarm thought. A man ought to be careful about what he put around his own neck.

Longarm deposited the voter record atop the Whig minute book and folded his arms across his chest. "Tell me, Sergeant, with the normal civil authority in Addington disrupted by the untimely death o' the chief here, which one o' us d'you think oughta take charge o' the investigation now?"

"We, uh, both could claim jurisdiction, couldn't we?" Braxton said.

"Yeah, I expect we both could. But we wouldn't wanta work crossways to one another, I'm sure."

"No, of course not." Braxton didn't really look so sure of that. "I was naturally assuming that as an officer of the state of Texas I would, um, take control of the continuing murder investigations."

"I c'n see how that'd be logical," Longarm acknowledged pleasantly. "Or we could go down t' the telegraph office an' send messages off t' our respective bosses. Ask, say, the U.S. attorney in Denver an' your top Ranger in Austin. What's his name again? Major Stone? I reckon we could ask him what t' do. In fact, that's likely a pretty good idea. I mean, I shouldn't put my nose in without an official request from some local or state officer, right? So let's just do it that way. We'll get a message off to Austin asking Major Stone what t' do here."

"I . . . don't think that will be necessary," Braxton said.

"No? What about the extension of jurisdiction here? I only have official authority when it comes t' the murder of the postmaster, y'know. I need somebody local . . ."

"I can make an official request for federal assistance on behalf of the Rangers," Braxton volunteered.

Which seemed to confuse the local cops all the more. And purely startled the hell out of several of the civilians who continued to mill about underfoot.

"Uh, Chuck . . . Deputy, that gentleman there is the vice mayor of Addington, Charles Henley . . . Chuck, why don't you make a formal request on behalf of the city that Deputy Marshal Long here, um, join us in the investigation into, uh, recent murders or other incidents of," he paused for a split second, a barely noticeable but rather telling delay, "incidents of violence."

Longarm damn near smiled about that. Limit the invitation to incidents of violence. Clever. Or so Braxton thought.

But then there were a couple of things that Longarm knew.

140

And that George Braxton did not know that Longarm knew.

Yeah, this was going to work out all right.

"Are you sure about this, George?"

"Chuck. Please. Trust me."

The vice mayor shrugged. "All right, if you say so." He turned to Longarm and said, "I hereby request that you assist us in the . . . how was that, George?"

"Assist in the investigation of recent murders and other acts of criminal violence."

"Yes. That." The vice mayor nodded briskly, then smiled and, like any politician, extended a hand so he could grab Longarm's hand and pump it.

"All right, gents. Thanks," Longarm said. "Now if you'll excuse me, I'm kinda tired. I'll see you'all in the morning. You," he pointed to one of the older police officers, "I'd like you t' arrange for the chief's body t' be cared for. An' did he have family? Yes? All right, then I'd like you," he pointed, "to break the news to them. That's something that oughta be done by somebody they know an' not a stranger. Mr. Vice Mayor, maybe you could go along to visit the family along with the officer, please? Thank you, sir. Is there anything else? No? Then I'll say good night."

He picked up the ledgers that Braxton had been trying to make off with and the police log too and walked out with all three of them under his arm.

Amos quietly followed. And once they were on the street and far out of hearing by the gentlemen back at City Hall, broke into laughter.

"That poor son of a bitch," Amos said. "I almost felt sorry for him."

"Yeah, I'll admit that I had Brass by the short hairs. An' he knew it."

"He's over here playing politics, the dumb bastard, and maybe his captain knows it and approves of it . . . that's something we'll want to look into later on . . . but I can guaran-damn-tee you the major doesn't know anything about it or Brass wouldn't be carrying a badge right now. Did you

141

see his face when you mentioned sending a wire to the major?''

Longarm nodded and grinned. ''Buckled his knees, didn't it?''

''I thought he was going to piss his britches there on the spot,'' Amos said.

''Right now he's hoping the Rangers never have to find out about his activities here. Not until or unless his cronies are in power in Austin. I expect then he'd feel safe.''

''He's going to have one hell of a surprise when he finds out there was another Ranger in that room watching him learn to crawl tonight.'' Amos' expression became more solemn. ''Come to think of it, Longarm, I guess I don't feel sorry for him after all. Guys like that give the rest of us a bad name.''

''No they don't, Amos. Because bad apples like that one get weeded out by good people like you and Major Stone.''

''You can count on that, my friend.''

''I do, Amos. I do.''

''Getting back to the main business at hand here, what do you think about Bender being murdered like that? Do you agree with that officer's theory that the chief had to know and trust whomever it was that shot him?''

''Looks that way on the surface, don't it,'' Longarm agreed in a too cheery tone of voice.

''Why do I get the impression you don't really mean that?'' Amos asked.

Longarm shrugged. And handed Amos the bulky ledgers he'd confiscated from Braxton. ''Do something t' keep these safe, will you? Me, I'm purely worn out. I got t' get some sleep else I'll be walking into walls soon.''

''Good night, Longarm.''

''G'night, Amo . . . Lester.''

Chapter 36

Longarm hadn't so much as had time to get through his breakfast before the locals began making courtesy calls. Courtesy hell, he realized. What they were doing was pleading for protection. Now that the police chief was dead, himself a victim of the unknown killer he had been sworn to apprehend, the Addington bigwigs were worried that their own asses might be on the line next. If J. Michael Bender could be shot down at his desk, then so could any of the rest of them. They knew it. And it scared the shit out of them.

"As mayor of this magnificent city," Hiram Worthington declared in a rich, mellow tone as if from a speaking dais, "I do concur with my vice mayor's action of last night, sir. I do hereby, and I might add quite heartily, request the assistance of the United States Justice Department and of you as a United States deputy marshal, sir, in upholding the laws of Texas and of this nation. And, um," he glanced about on all sides and lowered his voice considerably, "I would ask in particular that you protect the elected officials of our city and of this county."

"Anyone special that you have in mind?" Longarm asked, knowing damn good and well who the mayor was most interested in but curious as to whether he would admit it.

"Well, um, naturally I am concerned for the well-being of

143

all our officials and indeed of all our citizens.''

''But . . . ?''

''But I, uh, think perhaps the most vulnerable would be those in, ah, the highest and most exposed positions.''

''Namely?''

''Yes, well, uh, in truth, sir, I would suggest that as mayor . . .'' Worthington didn't want to complete the sentence. He did not want to seem the coward. On the other hand he was even less desirous of seeing himself bravely dead. He dropped his voice to a bare whisper and leaned close, hissing practically into Longarm's ear, ''Dammit, sir, I need protection.''

''Yes, sir, I think perhaps you do. And if I had any authority over the local police . . .''

''Is that what you want? Fine. I can, um, I can offer you a temporary appointment, complete with remuneration in the same amounts . . .''

''No pay,'' Longarm said. ''I draw my salary from the Justice Department. We don't take anything on the side, not for services rendered nor even rewards. That kinda keeps things on a even keel if you see what I mean.''

His honor the mayor seemed slightly disappointed to discover that he did not have the leverage of cash to apply to his own future welfare. But he recovered quickly enough. ''You would accept the appointment, though, if not the pay?''

''Yes, sir, I reckon I could do that for you.''

''Then consider yourself to be the new police chief pro tempore of Addington, Texas, Mr . . . excuse me, what is your name again?''

Longarm hid his amusement and settled for answering the question.

''Long. Yes. Of course.'' The mayor smiled. ''Deputy Long. Or perhaps I should say Chief Long, mm? I have the authority to make the appointment now on a temporary basis and we will convene a special meeting of the city council, say, tonight at eight o'clock in the second-floor chambers at City Hall. Your appointment will be confirmed then. You are, uh, welcome to attend if you wish. In fact, uh, I would be particularly grateful if you could be with me on a rather regular basis for the next few days and . . .''

"Mr. Mayor, excuse me for interrupting here, but I reckon I know what it is you're getting at. An' I got t' tell you, being a bodyguard, however valuable that service would be, ain't exactly what I come here t' do. Besides, guarding one fella would just tell our killer he should go after someone else as an easier target. No, what I gotta do is find out who's doing the shooting an' put a stop to it that way. Howsomever, sir, as chief o' police I expect I can assign one o' the duty officers to keep a special eye on you an' on the other, shall we say, more vulnerable folks.''

"That would be, uh, entirely acceptable, Chief.''

"Yes, sir. Now if you'll excuse me?''

The mayor left, and the duly appointed police chief pro tempore finished his breakfast with not more than three further interruptions by public and party officials who were worried about protecting their butts.

Once done with his meal he stopped at the hotel desk to ask that a tub and hot water be carried up to his room, then walked over to City Hall to inform the day shift that they had a new, albeit temporary boss, and to instruct them that the powers that be should be mollified with a show of interest on the part of the uniformed officers.

"Make yourselves conspicuous as hell,'' Longarm told the cops, all of whom had come in, including those who were not technically on duty at the moment. "You aren't expected to accomplish much. No killer in his right mind will try anything with you boys around. Which o' course is the whole idea. Keep the killer away by showing yourselves an' at that same time you'll be pleasing the fellas that come up with your pay. All right?''

The Addington police weren't really all that bad a bunch, Longarm thought. They couldn't much like the idea of a stranger taking over from their dead boss, but they were polite and didn't offer any public mutiny. That was about as good as he could have hoped, and he was satisfied with it.

"I got an appointment over at the hotel," he said without bothering to mention that his appointment was with a bathtub, "but I'll come back over later an' see what we can figure out about this mess. In the meantime if any o' you has any ideas about what we're looking for, get your thoughts in order 'cause I'll want t' hear your arguments soon as I get back. Okay?"

The cops seemed to like the idea of being consulted—Longarm had the impression that listening to the thoughts of his subordinates might not have been among Michael Bender's habits when he was chief—and were already conferring among themselves when Longarm departed.

When he got back to the hotel the desk clerk motioned him over.

"I hope you ain't gonna tell me that my bath isn't ready," he said.

"Not at all. Your tub and water are waiting for you. So is a visitor."

"Pardon me?"

"It seemed . . . inadvisable for this particular visitor to wait in the public lobby. Not seemly, if you know what I mean."

"No, I reckon I don't know what you mean."

"She said it was official business, deputy. She said she had to see you regarding an investigation?"

She, Longarm thought. Janie again. Damn, but that was one horny woman.

Well then, she could just scrub his back for him.

He supposed there were worse ways to spend a morning.

He thanked the clerk and started up the stairs.

Chapter 37

It was not Janie Sproul who greeted Longarm on his return to the hotel room but slim and vibrant Clarice. She was smiling hugely when she ran lightly across the room and flung herself onto him, demanding kisses and hugs.

"I have the day off and I got to thinking that . . . well . . . the first time was so nice that I thought we should do it again just to make sure I really do like it as much as I think I do," she told him.

Longarm chuckled and carried her over to the bed where he unceremoniously dumped her on her butt. "Some things oughta be checked out real careful before you reach conclusions," he agreed.

Clarice smiled. And began unfastening the buttons at her throat.

Longarm stroked the soft curls of her public hair, petting her there while he gently sucked and licked at her nipples. Clarice like that uncommonly well, and he'd discovered it was a sure-fire way to arouse the girl.

Not that either of them likely could stand much more in the way of arousal right now. He'd made it twice and she'd climaxed at least three times already. But the activity was still pleasant. And kind of friendly. He lightly stroked and licked while she fondled his limp, wet pecker and sighed repeatedly in his ear.

"You like?" he asked.

"Better than being with any old girl," she said. "Can I tell you something?"

"Um-hmm."

"I think I might not be a lesbian after all. Isn't that awful?"

"Oh, I don't think I'd call it awful. Hell, I think it's kinda nice."

Clarice shivered. "It sort of frightens me. I mean, all this time I've thought I knew who and what I was. Now I'm not sure at all. That is scary."

"I expect I can see how it would be. But let me tell you something, Clarice. You are one sweet, lovely, sexy lady. You got a lot t' offer. To anybody. You know what I'm telling you?"

She smiled and kissed him. "I think so. Thank you."

Longarm squeezed her tit and returned the kiss. "Tell you what."

"Yes?"

"By now that bath water is prob'ly cold as a fresh mountain stream in springtime, but me, I feel rank an' nasty as a old billy goat." He grinned. "And if you don't mind me mentioning it, lady, you don't smell like no petunia your own self. Let's wallow around in that tub a while. Then after, well, maybe we'll have recovered enough that we can have another go at makin' the beast with two backs one more time."

"Promise?" she asked.

"Promise."

Clarice laughed. "I'll scrub your back, dear, if you'll scrub mine."

"Deal," he said.

It was some considerable time afterward that, thoroughly sated, he lay on the bed with a cheroot in one hand and Clarice's soft tit in the other.

"I'm glad you got a day off," he said sleepily.

"Me too. Aunt Edith is so mad it's a wonder she doesn't spit. But I'm glad."

"What's she s' mad about?" Longarm asked.

"I'm really not sure. Something to do with Uncle Herbert."

"Oh, yes. I remember now. Herbert the black sheep. But I'd kinda got the impression he wasn't around much."

"He wasn't. Not for about as long as I can remember. He was away for simply years and years. Now he's back. At least I think he is. I haven't seen him, but I heard Aunt Edith talking last night, something about Uncle Herbert. I didn't hear what exactly. And then this morning when I got up she was already gone. Barb said she came downstairs in time to see Aunt Edith on her way out and when Barb asked about the store Aunt Edith said don't bother to open it—she didn't know when she would be back and she couldn't be bothered having to think about ice cream and stuff right then. That isn't at all like her. I've never known her to do anything like this, so it must be serious, whatever it is."

Longarm shrugged and puffed on his cigar, then after a moment he stroked the back of Clarice's head and nudged her in the direction of his right nipple. Damn but it felt fine when she got to work on that thing.

Chapter 38

Longarm hadn't any more than reached the street than they were on him like a flock of vultures on a week-dead burro.

"Are you the new police chief? You are, aren't you? Well, you have to do something about that awful Tommy Meacham. He's been peeking in at my little girl's bedroom window and . . ."

"Mr. Long, is it? I am Alice Fowler, Mr. Long, and my husband is a county commissioner, and I want to tell you a few things before you . . ."

"Could I have a moment of your time, sir? It's about a new line of uniforms, badges and fancy leather goods of the very highest quality, and they are all available to you and to the members of your fine department at discount rates that . . ."

"Just want you t' know, chief, that you and your boys are always welcome at the Red Cat. If you don't know where it is, why, you just ask anybody. Six girls working every night, chief. More on weekends. And if you want something special you can ask for . . ."

"Lewis. His name is Lewis Peabody, and I know he is the one stealing eggs from my hen house. The only reason I haven't caught him at it is because he's so clever, but I know if you set your mind to it . . ."

"Chief?" The voice was low and even. And came from a cop in uniform.

"Yes, uh," he had to reach for the memory after such hurried introductions earlier, "what is it, Tyler?"

"We got a confrontation over at the Muddy Waters, Chief. I think you'd best handle it."

Longarm excused himself from all the flies that were buzzing around him—they really weren't so bad as vultures, after all—and followed the officer down the main avenue and up one of the narrow cross streets. The Muddy Waters turned out to be a small but rather nicely appointed saloon.

At the moment, however, what would normally be a pleasant and welcoming atmosphere was marred somewhat by a taut standoff between two very nervous men, each of whom held a revolver awkwardly at waist level.

"By God, Jennings, you lay that thing down on the bar and walk away."

"Turn my back on you, Henry? Damned if I will. You and your people shoot decent folk in cold blood. I'll give you no chance to do it to me."

"Afternoon, gents," Longarm put in from the vicinity of the doorway. "That's good thinking. Keep your eyes on the other fellow, each o' you. Don't look away for more'n a split second lest the other'n up an' fire," he advised in a soft voice. "When you can, I want you each t' glance this way. Just for a second. You see who I am?"

Despite the advice he had just given the two would-be combatants, each quite naturally looked to see who the hell it was who was talking like that.

Which he had fully expected they would, in fact.

He nodded pleasantly first to one and then to the other. "G'on back t' watching each other now. Gotta be careful, y'know. Would somebody mind telling me who these fellas are that're fixing to bloody up the floor in here?"

"I'm Randal Jennings, Marshal." He held himself stiffly erect with his chin belligerently extended in the direction of his opponent. "I am county chairman of the Whig party, sir."

"County assassin is more like it," the other fellow claimed.

"An' you would be . . . ?"

"Henry Brightwax, Chief. Elected head of the east Texas district of the Democratic party. And one of his intended victims, I'm sure." Brightwax motioned with his free hand toward the Whig who opposed him. In more ways at the moment than merely politically.

"I take it you boys are having a difference of opinion about something?" Longarm suggested.

"He knows what it's about," Brightwax claimed.

"Lying piece of shit," Jennings returned. "It's your bunch that's behind all this . . ."

"Whoa, dammit," Longarm said, eyeing the guns the two were holding.

And holding rather inexpertly, he thought. Time to put a stop to this bull.

"Now I know you both mean what you say," he told them, "and I'm sure you each have good reason for doing what you are doing here. So what I'm gonna do is ask all these other fellas in the place t' move aside an' give you boys plenty o' room to settle your business. That's right, everybody over onta this side o' the room. You too, bartender. Come out from behind there for a minute. We don't want anybody hurt by stray bullets."

"What?"

"It's all right. Man has a right t' defend his honor, his woman, his property or his dog, that's the way I see it. If you boys wanta blow holes in one another, I won't try an' stop you. Mostly because I couldn't. Y'know? I mean, if I try an' take one o' you, then the other'd be free t' fire away when my back was turned. That wouldn't be fair. Wouldn't be at all right. No, I can't handle but the one o' you at a time. So what I'm gonna do, I think, is let you fellas go ahead an' fight it out. Like as not that means one o' you will be dead pretty soon."

Oh, he did have their attention now. Theirs and that of every other man in the place. Longarm took a couple steps forward, clear of the crowd behind him, and without any rush or hurry dragged the big Colt out of his crossdraw holster, holding it pointed in the general direction of the ceiling so everyone—especially Jennings and Brightwax—could get a good look at the weapon.

His double-action Colt would fire perfectly well with a single pull of the trigger. But there was something nice and dramatic about the smooth, oiled *cla-clack* of a well-fitted hammer being drawn back into a full-cock position.

And the room was damn sure quiet enough for everyone to hear.

Longarm drew the hammer of the Colt back nice and slow, letting everyone in on the fact.

"T' make this fair," he said, "I'll count t' three. You're each free t' aim an' fire at the count o' three. All right? Then after . . . you got t' remember that dueling is outlawed in this whole country, by federal law that is . . . then after you boys shoot . . . I got to tell you that it will be my bounden duty as a sworn peace officer, both o' the United States gummint an' now of the town of Addington, Texas, also . . . when you boys are done shooting, I will have t' arrest whichever one of you is the survivor. You'll forgive me, I hope, but I didn't stay a peace officer this long by taking chances, an' one of you boys will be standing there, a criminal sure as hell, with a loaded gun in his hand an' me having to arrest him. Which I will be duty bound t' do. So what I got t' explain t' you both is that while one o' you will have the satisfaction of blowing a hole in the guts o' the other an' winning his point by force of manly arms, that same one is gonna have to be taken down by me right after. One o' you will be dead in the sawdust on this floor here, an' the other one I will not take no chances with. What I will have t' do soon as you boys are done shooting at one another, I will protect myself and all these innocent bystanders by shooting whoever is left standing. An' if I do say so my own self, I am a pretty good shot with this here Colt gun so I will aim careful an' you won't feel hardly a thing. A

153

hard thump on the head an' it'll be over. All right? You boys ready? One . . ."

"Wait, wait, now wait a damn minute."

"Jesus, Marshal, you can't mean . . ."

"It's clear as clear can be," Longarm said agreeably. "You boys take care of business, then I take down whichever one o' you is left. Real simple."

"But that means we would both die!" Jennings yelped.

"Oh, I dunno," Longarm said. "The one I shoot will be cold meat pretty certain, but there's always a chance that the other fella will get over his wounds." He shook his head as if in great admiration. "It's purely amazing what a human person can stand an' keep on living. Hell, I've seen fellas with their jaws shot clean off, others with holes you could push a fist through in the lungs, or if you're hit in the balls you near always live. You can have your pecker shot clean off an' hardly even need much time to heal. You wouldn't think that, but it's true."

Neither Jennings nor Brightwax looked so eager to deliver the other a comeuppance any longer.

In fact, Longarm thought they were commencing to look just the least bit pale, each of them.

"Are you ready now? One . . ." What the hell was he going to do if they let him keep counting? he suddenly, and rather terrifyingly, thought. "Two . . ."

"Jesus, Marshal, can't you give us a minute to think about this?"

"Oh, hell yes. I'm sorry. I just thought . . ."

"Dammit, Henry, I'll lay mine down if you'll lay yours down too."

"I'd lay mine down, Randal."

"Both of us at the same time then?"

"Yeah, but . . . not on the count of three. Let's just kind of reach out . . . like that, yeah, and lay them on the bar. Easy now. Easy does it. And . . . oh, jeez."

Both men looked limp and purely wrung out as if they'd just passed through a great and unsettling ordeal.

As perhaps in fact they had.

Longarm managed to look disappointed as he uncocked the Colt and returned it to its holster.

"Bartender, I think it'd be a good idea if you'd pour some drinks now," he said. "Startin' with those fellas over there, eh?"

Chapter 39

If he had let them, the politicians and powers that be likely would have kept him occupied half the night long. Or longer. And he simply was not interested in putting himself through that. The silly sons of bitches talked exhaustively, endlessly, about nothing at all. And all of it so intense and serious that if you didn't listen closely you might actually think they were saying something.

Even before they got around to formally naming him acting police chief, Longarm gave up and slipped away to the hotel.

He left word at the desk that he was not in. Not to the mayor, not to Judge Sproul's widow, not to any-damn-body.

Then he went upstairs and got the best, and earliest, night's sleep he'd had in he couldn't remember how long.

Come morning he ate in the kitchen. He tried sitting down to a normal table in the restaurant but was so overwhelmed with people coming by to ask, to bitch, to worry or simply to talk that he soon enough gave up on that and carried his plate into the kitchen where it was hot and noisy and crowded. But where at least he could eat his meal without interruption.

He could not say the same about the routine at City Hall. Once he sat down behind the police chief's desk he was fair game for any citizen who wanted to pester him.

And he would have sworn that a clear majority of the Addington populace was intent on having "a few minutes of your time, sir, that's all I ask." And all of them on this one short morning.

Being chief of police amid a bunch of damn busybodies proved not as easy as Longarm might have thought. For certain sure not as easy as he would have hoped.

Hell, there was one poor woman who in all seriousness accused her neighbor of eavesdropping on her. By way of the neighbor's house cat.

"It spies on me, you know. It's true. It really does."

"Then what I suggest you do, ma'am, is bribe the cat to spy on the neighbor for you," he told her back, just as serious and solemn as he knew how.

"Oh, I couldn't do a thing like that."

"No? Then have you considered talking to the pharmacist about a good poison?"

"My neighbor *is* the only pharmacist in town, sir."

"Then go to the hardware store and ask about a trap, ma'am."

"Goodness, I hadn't thought about that. Thank you." She smiled brightly. And then added a regretful little frown on the end of it. "Such a shame. I do like pussies."

"Yes, ma'am," Longarm said. "So do I."

"Thank you, Chief Long. You have been a big help to me. I will never forget you."

"Yes, ma'am." She toddled out of the office with the aid of a cane and went painfully down the staircase. Longarm rolled his eyes and tried to prepare himself for the ordeal of his next visitor.

It was, however, the older day officer—Longarm had already decided to name the man a sergeant and make him responsible for this routine horse-hooey—who came into the office.

"Yes, Baines?"

"Got another death in town, chief."

"Not . . . ?"

157

"No, sir, not another murder. This one looks like an accidental drowning."

Longarm grunted. Things like that were regrettable but essentially unpreventable. Still, it was a shame. "Not a politician, I hope."

"No, sir. A spinster lady. Edith Matthews. Runs . . . that is to say she used to run . . . the ice cream parlor in town."

Clarice's aunt. That caught Longarm's attention.

"You say she drowned?"

"Yes, sir. A couple kids snuck away to see could they catch some fish. What they found was Miss Edith floating in an eddy about three quarters of a mile south of town."

"Which makes it officially outside our jurisdiction, right?" Longarm asked.

"Yes, sir. Not that it has to come under anybody's jurisdiction, it being accidental and all. The justice of the peace will hold an inquest by and by, and the estate will go through probate."

"There is a county coroner, I presume."

"Sure, but I doubt anyone will bother calling him in on it. I mean, it's plain enough how she died."

"Uh-huh."

"Funny thing, though."

"What's that?"

"Miss Edith was always one to keep to herself. Real quiet, her and her relatives. Bunch of women living all alone in a big house."

"Yes?"

"Quiet, like I said. But just this morning she made something of a spectacle of herself at Bryce Peabody's place. Poor thing. And now she's dead." The soon-to-be sergeant shook his head in sympathy. "I wonder if the old girl took to nipping at the laudanum or vanilla extract or something of the like."

"It happens," Longarm agreed. "What was this about her making a . . . spectacle, did you say?"

"That's sure the way I'd put it. Bryce . . . he's a mule

158

trader, mind: Lived here all his life . . . he woke up about five o'clock this morning to what he thought sounded like somebody scuffling on his front porch.''

''Oh?''

''He said he was scared it was the killer come for him. But shit, Bryce isn't anybody. Just a sorry-ass mule trader with a bunch of kids he can't hardly keep in shoes. Not the sort our killer would want at all.''

''Uh-huh.''

''I guess Bryce was scared anyway. He isn't real brave and never has been. He got up and looked out the front window. Said he saw the bushes waving around like crazy, and up on the porch there was Miss Edith. He knew she wasn't no threat to anybody. Hell, she's never had any use for any man. So he went and opened the door to ask what she was doing out there making all that noise, and she jumped down into the bushes and ran off before he could ask her anything or so much as speak to her. Said she seen him and took off running like she was a filly half her age. Now the poor old thing turns up dead. I wouldn't wonder if she had a heart attack from running away from Bryce and fell over dead into the river. What do you think?''

''Edith Matthews, you said her name is?''

''That's right.''

''Then I'll tell you what I think, Baines. I think I want you to find this Bryce Peabody and tell him I want to talk to him. Right away. And once you've got Peabody pointed this way, I'd like you to find Norman Colton's cousin Lester and tell him that I need to see him too. Can do?''

The officer gave his new chief a look that questioned Longarm's good sense. But then the boss, right or wrong, is always the boss. ''Right away, Chief.''

''Thanks, Baines.''

''Yes, sir. Uh, should I send the next visitor in while you're waiting for Bryce to get here?''

Longarm sighed. ''I s'pose we might as well get through as many as we can. Send 'im in.''

159

Baines grinned. "Her. The next one is a her, sir. And if you thought Mrs. Lucas was nuts, wait until you talk to this one."

Mrs. Lucas was the lady whose neighbor's cat spied on her. The man who might—or might damn well not—become sergeant was laughing when he walked out the door.

Chapter 40

"Come in, Lester."

Amos Vent gave a mildly puzzled look at the skinny man in the straw hat and bib overalls who was just leaving the police chief's office.

"You might oughta shut the door," Longarm suggested.

Amos helped himself to the chair Longarm had put in front of the desk for the convenience of visitors—he was thinking of replacing it with a rack and thumbscrew instead but didn't know if the city budget would allow for the purchase; it was something he would certainly have wanted to check out if he had to stay here for any length of time—and shook his head at Longarm's offer of a cheroot.

"Mind if I light up?" The question was hardly a serious one. Longarm's match was aflame almost before he'd finished asking it.

"Your subordinate said you wanted to see me, oh great white chief?"

Longarm grinned and flicked his match, still burning, in Amos' general direction. "Damn good thing you jumped t' obey too or I'd've had you in irons."

"That's why I came in such a hurry."

"Tell me, Amos, d'you have everything you need on our good friend Sergeant Braxton?"

"Everything the major could want," Amos confirmed. "It's pretty clear he was working on behalf of a political party and not for the state of Texas or the Ranger force."

Longarm grunted.

"He knew where those books were and he wanted to keep them for whatever use Bender had them."

"Stole them," Longarm corrected.

"Yeah, that's the way I see it. Though I suppose we won't ever know if it was Bender himself that knocked into you in the dark that night or if it was one of his Texas First henchmen. For sure, they were behind it. Behind the killings then too, I'd say."

Longarm shook his head though. "Not at all, Amos. Bender and his people were plenty happy to take advantage of the killings when they happened. But it wasn't them or the Whigs who are behind the murders."

"Can't be the Democratics then, can it? I don't see how they'd fit into . . ."

"Not them either," Longarm told him.

"But shit, old pard, it pretty much has to be one of them, doesn't it?"

"Matter o' fact, Amos, it doesn't."

"You wanta explain that?"

"Amos, it was told to me straight out, right after I got here. But you and me, we was so intent on finding conspiracy that we never considered the plain and simple. The killer is a stupid, prideful son of a bitch named Buddy Matthews. Herbert Matthews for the proper version of it. He got out of jail recently an' has been wandering around getting revenge on the people that he thinks are responsible for ruining his life."

"That's the fellow that judge's widow told you about."

"That's the one," Longarm agreed.

"But what about . . . ?"

"Politics had nothing t' do with it, Amos. It just happened that some of the fellows of that age and social background grew into positions high on the social ladder around here. But hell, that's only natural considering who them and their fam-

162

ilies were, most of them, and the time that's passed since. If this Matthews hadn't gone to prison, with his record as a war hero and being from an old family, he prob'ly would've been he-coon of one party or another around here his own self. But think about it. The first fellow to be killed, Wil Meyers, he wasn't anybody of consequence in the community. We been overlooking the implications o' Meyers' death an' concentrating on the positions o' the later victims like Norman Colton an' Deel and now Chief Bender. But they were all of an age and all from pretty much the same background. An' the lucky fella that just left here, a mule trader name of Peabody, confirmed to me just now that every one o' those ol' boys took part in a silly damn shivaree year an' years ago. One that went wrong when some tempers got outa hand that night. Tempers that aren't all under control even yet.''

"What does Peabody have to do with it?"

"He would have been the next victim, I'm sure, except Herbert Matthews' sister stopped him. I don't have witnesses to that. Not yet. But I'd just about swear to it. She stopped him on Peabody's porch before dawn an' then she took off after him. Wanted to keep him from disgracing the family any further, I suppose. My guess is that the woman caught up with him down along the river and either he killed her outright or she got so worked up she had a heart attack or maybe just fell in the water and drowned. Whatever, our boy Buddy Matthews is out there somewhere not far away. It won't be any great trick t' find him and put him back behind the high walls.''

"You want me to back you up, my friend?"

"No need, Amos. That's what I wanted t' tell you here. This whole thing is simpler than we thought. I want you t' concentrate on cleaning up your Ranger Company F—Braxton for sure but who knows who else might've been in on this deal—and making sure the Texas First party does everything nice an' legal.''

"Even though they are trying to secede from the Union?" Amos asked.

"Shit, my friend, if they can do it legal, it wouldn't gravel me none t' be without Texas as one o' the states. Be just that much less for me t' worry about policing. Y'know?'' He grinned.

"Do you need those ledgers you confiscated from Braxton?''

"I c'n do without 'em if you want to take them along t' show the major.''

Amos nodded and stood. "Are you sure you don't want me to stick around a while longer and back you against this Matthews fellow?''

Longarm chuckled, "What is it you Rangers like t' claim? One Ranger, one mob. Isn't that it?''

Amos nodded. "Something like that, yes.''

"Then maybe one deputy marshal can limp along after one ex-con.''

Amos extended his hand. "Come by Austin when you're done, Longarm. The major will at least want a deposition from you, I'm sure. We'll have to let him decide if he needs courtroom testimony from you. If it comes to that.''

"If it does I expect I'll be wherever a subpoena tells me t' be.''

"Good luck to you.''

"And t' you, my friend.''

Amos left, and Longarm called Baines into the office. He needed directions to a place called Avondale. And before that he supposed he should visit Janie Sproul. With luck she might still have a picture of her first husband. If not, then a description would just have to do.

Chapter 41

Avondale smelled like shit. Chicken shit, actually. The place was swarming with chickens. Chickens in pens. Chickens in coops. Chickens under-damn-foot. There were chickens, and chicken shit, in every direction. And the smell of all those chickens was enough to make a man swear off ham and eggs for the remainder of his natural life.

The locals, what few of them there were, quite naturally seemed immune to the stink. But then, they would be so accustomed to it that they probably no longer smelled it on any conscious level.

Longarm wished he was so fortunate. He wrinkled his nose and ducked low to clear the doorway of a shack—but then every structure he could see in Avondale was a shack or no better than one—that had a crude sign tacked over the door announcing something in a weird-looking writing that Longarm couldn't recall ever seeing before and, in smaller and even more crudely written letters, the lone English word—or so he assumed—"booz."

There were three men inside: a bartender and two customers. All three looked like they might have come out of the same mold. Short, stockily built, round red cheeks, huge mustaches and shocks of wildly unruly hair. All wore overalls and faded red union suits. There didn't seem to be a shoe or a boot among them. Which he considered one hell of a handicap considering all the chicken shit decorating the ground outside.

Come to think of it, there was a good amount of the stuff on the floor of the place too, no doubt dragged in by years of visits from shitty customers.

The bartender looked at him and asked a question in a language Longarm didn't even recognize, much less understand. What had Janie said—Hungarian?

"Any o' you boys speak English?"

No one responded.

Shit! he thought.

He pulled out his wallet—always a good way to attract some interest in a cheap dump like this—and flipped it open to display his badge.

The reaction was immediate.

The bartender developed both a frightened look and an ability to comprehend English.

And the two customers muttered their apologies and made a hasty departure.

"Sorry about scarin' off all your trade," Longarm apologized. Hell, he meant it. He hadn't come here to cause any hurt to anybody. Well, not anybody local anyhow.

"Nothing, sir, I have done nothing, I tell you true." The poor saloonkeeper looked like he was going to add a dump of his own to the shit already on the floor. "I obey all law, sir, every one, yes."

The poor sap pulled a cigar box out from under the counter, opened it, and extended it to Longarm.

Damn thing held a couple lousy bucks in very small change. Likely it was all he'd taken in for days past.

"Mister, I didn't come here to rob you."

"No rob. I give. Good citizen, yes. You take. Please." He looked ready to cry. "Take. Please. Don' hurt . . . you know." He motioned vaguely toward the back of the shanty. Maybe he had some family back there, Longarm figured.

The man acted like he thought any lawman, cop, or public official who came in was apt to steal his money, burn his place

166

down, who the hell knew what else.

It was a reaction Longarm had seen before in immigrants from certain unbeloved Old Country pasts. And one that quite frankly sickened him whenever he saw it anew.

Folks should always have the right to expect protection from the people given positions of civil authority.

But apparently it wasn't always exactly that way in all parts of the world.

Blessings, Longarm thought then as he had before. Some of us forget to count them.

It took him a couple of minutes to convince the man that Longarm hadn't come there to rob or intimidate or otherwise to harm him.

"I'm looking for a fella name of Buddy Matthews. Herbert Matthews, actually." He pulled out the fading daguerreotype Janie'd dug up for him and showed it to the saloonkeeper. "This picture is awful old, but you might recognize him anyway."

"Yes, sure. Mr. Buddy. He come in. Drink some. Spend a little money. Never happy though. I never see him smile, not one time."

"You do know him though."

"Yes, sure. Nice fella, Mr. Buddy." The bartender bared his teeth behind a curtain of mustache hairs.

"Yeah. Nice," Longarm said dryly. "You know where he is now? Where I can find him today?"

"Sure thing, yes. Last night he spend all his money here. Big drunk. You know? Say it don' matter if he broke. Say he gonna go home an' get some more. Home." The bartender frowned. "I don' know where his home is though."

"That's all right. I do."

"Mr. Officer, you really not going to . . . you know?"

"Friend, you been a big help t' me. You got nothing t' fear from me. Not never." Longarm laid a silver dollar on the bar as compensation for the trade he'd run off. At least that was what he told himself it was for.

Then he turned and headed back for Addington. With luck, he figured, he could be there before dark.

Chapter 42

Nobody home. Dammit anyhow, there seemed to be nobody home at the tall old house where Edith Matthews and family lived.

He tapped once again on the front-door windowpane, then reared back and gave the sturdier wooden part of the door a couple solid whacks just to make sure no one inside could have missed his knock.

Still there was no response.

If Matthews was in there . . . he supposed he could go and get a warrant if he had to. Surely the local JP would accommodate the new police chief.

But he would hate to leave and give Matthews an opportunity to slip away if the man was inside.

Longarm thought it over and decided if necessary he would get one of the neighbors or pay a kid to go downtown and find a police officer. That way Longarm could get the cop to fetch the warrant while he himself kept watch at the house.

But then, dammit, he didn't know for certain sure that Herbert Buddy Matthews was in fact inside.

On impulse he tried the door knob.

It was locked. Which removed temptation, however. He supposed that was something.

But it didn't get the job done. And what he really needed to do was find out if there was reason enough to get the warrant and violate these folks' privacy on the same day the leader of their clan, such as it was, got herself killed.

Which, come to think of it, he found kinda strange now. There should have been people scurrying in and out like a nest of ants. Edith Matthews was dead. So where were all the mourners, all the neighbors, all the good churchgoing folk who should be here with their pies and platters, their hams and fried chickens and deviled eggs and angel food cakes?

There was something damned strange about the Matthews house being locked and silent on this of all days.

Hell, even if everybody in Addington knew about the aberrant lifestyle of Edith and her nieces, people still should have come.

If for no other reason, they'd come so they could congratulate themselves afterward on how Christian and understanding they all were.

No, this really wasn't making sense now that he thought on it.

He tried the door again, harder this time, but that didn't do a thing to change the fact that it was locked.

And there were curtains pulled at all the windows. He checked, stalking back and forth along the porch where he'd once sat and shared a lemonade with Clarice, but every window was carefully covered.

Had they been covered the other day when he was here? He couldn't remember.

It hadn't seemed important at the time.

He tried peering into the side windows, but they were covered too. Every one of them.

He went around back to the little laundry porch and mounted the stairs there. The back door was locked and the small glass pane in that window covered.

Damn it, anyway.

The right and logical and proper thing to do now, of course, would be for him to leave. Or if he really felt he had to look inside the house, send for an officer and eventually a proper search warrant.

Right. That was the correct thing to do. No doubt about it.

Longarm left the back porch and looked around inside a tool and storage shed in the back yard. After a few moments he found what he wanted.

He took the scrap of rusted wire and straightened it, then bent a short hook at a right angle on one end.

With that for a key he returned to the back door of the Matthews house and began burgling the place.

Chapter 43

Oh, shit. Longarm swallowed. Hard. Sweet Jesus!

The short hall between the kitchen and dining room ran thick with blood. Tacky, copper-smelling, none too old blood.

He couldn't see the source, but he could sure as hell see the blood.

There wasn't any way to avoid it, none that he knew of, so he walked through it, conscious of the sticky-slippery texture underfoot, into the entry hall.

He could see then where all the blood was coming from.

Barbara. The short, plump, cheerful little waitress he remembered from that visit to Edith Matthews's ice cream parlor. Clarice's cousin Barbara.

She lay on the dining-room floor like a cast-off doll that had lost its stuffing. She seemed awfully small and . . . empty . . . lying there with an enormous, gaping hole where her throat should have been.

She was dressed in her work uniform. Perhaps she'd just come back from . . . except no, her aunt was killed that morning. More likely she'd been dressed ready to go to work when she heard that news and then never got around to changing clothes since.

Or there could be a hundred other perfectly reasonable explanations. Longarm likely would never know the truth of it.

The truth he did know about was that the girl's throat had been horribly slashed, the cut so deep it very nearly severed her head from her body.

He looked at her and shuddered.

In the parlor there was another body. A mature woman with a faint resemblance to Edith. The other aunt Clarice had told him about? Possible. Or a neighbor. Friend. One of Edith's lovers. Somebody in town would know.

Damn it.

Longarm drew his Colt and held it at the ready while he moved ghost-quiet through the rest of the downstairs.

There were no other bodies.

Only two. *Only.* Jeez. Murder was bad enough. Murdering women was worse. Two women dead in this house.

And no sign of Clarice.

He should have found Clarice. Barbara was here. And the woman he thought was the other aunt. So where the hell was Clarice?

Longarm held his revolver in his left hand for a moment while he slowly and carefully wiped his right palm—damp with dread—on a trouser leg; then he resumed his grip on the gun.

And began slowly carefully mounting the steps toward the bedroom where he and Clarice had romped. So very few days past.

He remembered the way.

Chapter 44

He heard the squeaking of bedsprings first.

And then after that the low, soft sobbing of a woman in tears.

They were in Clarice's bedroom.

The door, he found, was primly shut.

Everyone else in the house was supposed to be dead, but Buddy Matthews had tidily closed the bedroom door before he began raping his niece.

Longarm twisted the knob, pulling the door slightly to him so as to release the latch with as little noise as possible. The brass tongue slipped free from the mortise without a sound, and Longarm breathed easier.

He could hear Clarice's weeping clearly now. And the steady, rhythmic creak of the springs along with the moist, meaty sound of flesh slapping flesh as two sweaty bellies collided over and over and over again.

Longarm made sure the Colt was comfortable in his hand and then pushed, ever so gently, on the door.

A groan of metal rubbing on metal sounded as the hinges objected.

It sounded almighty loud in Longarm's ears. But then from inside the room, to someone distracted as Matthews no doubt was by now . . .

He pushed the door open another few inches and slipped inside.

To find Buddy Matthews, trousers around his ankles and his boots still on but his ass bare and pale, shiny in the yellow lamplight inside Clarice's half-darkened room.

The man was lodged deep between Clarice's legs, covering her slim body with his own.

The two had stopped their movement at the intrusion.

Both looked at him with the wild, wide-eyed stares of deer caught unexpectedly in the beam of a bull's-eye lantern.

Both seemed frozen in place, locked into position with Clarice spread open to the lust of her own uncle.

Except they hadn't become frozen quite quickly enough.

Matthews must have had excellent hearing and perfect reflexes too, for with so little warning he had grabbed a slim, long-barreled revolver—Longarm recognized the gun as a crude Colt replica from the old cap-and-ball days, probably one of the weapons so hastily manufactured for the Confederacy by Dance Brothers or Griswold and Greer or some similar, even less well-known makeshift factory—and was holding it tight to Clarice's temple.

The girl looked at Longarm, and her tears flowed anew.

Her uncle held the cocked revolver tight to Clarice's head with one hand and with the other quite casually reached over onto the nightstand beside her bed.

He picked up a blood-crusted folding razor—no wonder the wounds in the flesh of the dead women downstairs had been so awful—and smiled at Longarm as he flipped the blade out of the handle and laid the edge ever so lightly across Clarice's throat.

"Move and she dies, Deputy."

"Do you know me?" Longarm asked.

"By reputation. I know who you are. I seen you at night sometimes lately. Know what else? I seen you screw with Clarey here. I got awful horny watching you do it with her. Those other bitches, they never liked being with boys. Not even when they were little. But Clarey, she likes a prick. Don't you, honey?''

When the girl did not answer, Matthews's voice hardened, and he repeated the question in a menacing hiss. "I said you like a prick. Don't you"

"Yes, I . . . yes I do."

"You like it when I screw you, don't you?"

"Yes, I like it."

"You like me screwing you better than you like him. Don't you."

"Yes."

"A lot."

"Yes, I like it a lot." Her voice was small, and the tears coursed freely down her cheeks to soak into the pillow behind her head.

Matthews's razor fluttered rapidly up and down with the wild cadence of the heartbeat in Clarice's throat.

"Don't . . . hurt me . . . please."

"You don't want me to do you like I did those bitches downstairs?"

"No. Please."

"I'll do whatever I damn want with you. You know that, don't you."

"Yes."

"And you respect me for that."

"Yes. Of course."

"You respect me a whole lot. Don't you."

"Yes. A lot."

"A *whole* lot," he corrected.

"A whole lot," she said obediently.

Longarm wondered if he could put one into the side of Matthews's head solidly enough—could you keep a dead man's hand from squeezing a trigger or from reflexively yanking downward with a damned razor?

The Colt . . . Shit, if he fired, he was more apt to kill Clarice than to save her. One movement of a single finger, and the girl would be dead. So would Matthews, but the hell with that.

Longarm had the rest of Herbert Matthews's life to kill him. The question was how much time Clarice had left to her young life.

"You did all right in prison before," Longarm said in a calm, conversational tone of voice. It was a lie, of course. The man might or might not have been very tightly strung together before he went behind the wall. For sure he'd come apart while he was in there.

The man was crazy as a june bug on a griddle. Completely round the bend.

He looked at Longarm and laughed.

And then, incredibly, he went back to screwing Clarice. While Longarm stood there aiming a revolver at him, Herbert Matthews went back to raping his niece.

He couldn't move that much without the effort of it jostling the hand that held the razor and after a few seconds blood began to spread over Clarice's neck. Not a lot of it at first. The cuts were small, but nearly every thrust of Matthews's cock into Clarice resulted in another tiny addition to the growing series of wounds and soon her neck and pillow were a bright, menacing scarlet.

Matthews saw. And laughed. "What do you think, Long? Should I finish the job? One slice. You know? You think I can get her head to drop off with one cut? How many? Do you want to make a bet on it? I say I can take it off with one push. What kind of wager do you want to put up?"

Longarm felt sick.

"Look, we can make a deal here, Matthews. You say you know my reputation. If you do, then you know I keep my word. Even to cons."

"That's what they say about you, all right. Everybody says Longarm, he's one pure son of a bitch. But he's square. He'll give a man a break if he can. He won't shoot unless he has to. And he keeps his word. That's what they say about you. They do."

"Then let's deal, Matthews. You and me. We work this out peaceable. You let Clarice go, and . . ."

"Dammit, Longarm, I get to finish with her first. I haven't had a chance to come in her yet. I got to do that first."

"Fine. But you let her go, Matthews."

"And then you let me go too, right?"

"I'll give you a head start, yes."

"Not good enough. You have to let me go." The man resumed stroking in and out of Clarice, slowly this time and rather absently while he seemed to concentrate mostly on his conversation with Longarm.

"Trying to catch me in a lie, Matthews? You know as well as I do that I wouldn't just let you go. I'll come after you. We both know that. But we can negotiate a head start. I'll give you that much in exchange for Clarice's life. You leave her be, and I'll give you two hours. If you cut her, Matthews, you're dead before you have time to stand up. You know that's true. I'll blow your head off your goddamn shoulders and laugh when I put the rest of the slugs into the corpse. Unless you let Clarice go. Two hours, Matthews. Or I kill you where you lie. Your choice, man. Call it."

"Twelve hours," Matthews countered.

"No chance. Two."

"Six."

"I might go three. No more."

"Hell with you, Long. Six."

"Three."

"Five, then."

"Four."

"Done. Yeah, four hours. But the time don't start until I'm done with ol' Clarice here. I get to finish my fun with her."

"If you hurt her, man, the deal is off. Cross me and I'll gutshoot you, Matthews. You'll take days t' die an' wish somebody'd have the Christian charity t' finish you sooner. But I won't let them. You hear me, man? Cross me and you'll die slow, and harder than you'd ever think possible."

"Four hours. You promised."

"Four hours. And you leave Clarice alive. You promised that."

Matthews laughed and used the knife hand to motion Longarm away. The muzzle of the revolver, though, never waved from the girl's temple. A few ounces of pressure, even accidental pressure, and her brains would be splattered all over the wall. "Go on now, Long. I wanta finish here, and I don't want you staring at me while I'm having my fun."

Longarm looked at Clarice and raised an eyebrow. She was scared, but she was brave enough too. She gave him a barely perceptible nod.

Longarm eased back from the door, leaving it ajar.

He hated to do it. But Clarice had only the slimmest of slim chances for life. Her uncle was quite thoroughly mad and anything might set him off beyond reason or rational control.

Within seconds he heard the creaking of the bed springs resume and, a minute or two after, begin to pound with furious rapidity.

He heard Matthews moan and Clarice cry out—in pain, he thought, not a shared pleasure—and then there was the sound of someone standing and moving about in the room.

That and a low, murmured whispering.

"No!" It was Clarice's voice. "I won't. You can't. Please Uncle Herbert. Don't take me. Don't make me . . . "

Longarm shoved the door open and came in, gun first.

Matthews, damn him, once again anticipated what was happening and already had the muzzle of his old-fashioned revolver pressed tight to Clarice's head just behind and below her ear.

"We have a deal," Matthews snarled.

"Clarice stays here. That's part of the deal."

"I changed my mind." In a taunting singsong as if they were a couple of small children disagreeing in a sandbox Matthews sang, "Nanny-nanny-woo-woo, I changed my my-ind, my my-ind, my my-ind."

He ended the insane ditty by sticking his tongue out at Longarm and bursting into laughter.

Clarice began to tremble violently, to shake and quiver as

178

her uncle held her at the throat with one hand and pressed the gun to her head with the other.

Clarice reached behind her. Longarm thought she was fumbling on the night stand for the razor. And perhaps she was. Matthews had not put it back there, however, and her blindly searching fingers found only bare wood.

And then the base of the oil lamp.

Longarm thought she would leave be then.

Dammit, he could still get Matthews to let her go.

He was sure of it.

But Clarice . . . she was not. Or so it seemed.

Her patience had worn out or her faith in Longarm's ability to free her . . . whatever other reason there might have been. He would never know. She grabbed. Turned. Lashed out.

The lamp shattered and whale oil spilled onto the bed, the curtains, onto Herbert Matthews and onto Clarice as well.

The oil caught fire, the flame spreading with a whoosh, and within seconds that entire side of the room was engulfed in an inferno.

Buddy Matthews screamed. He jumped up and down, beating at his burning clothes with hands that quickly scorched and blistered. His hair caught fire, and the man began to shriek in agony.

Longarm dashed forward.

"Help me. For God's sake help me," Matthews cried.

Longarm bent. Grabbed. Ignored the pain that shot through his hands and arms.

He grabbed Clarice. Threw her hard onto the floor and pulled up one edge of the heavy oriental rug there to wrap her in and smother the flames that already covered most of her slim, fragile body.

"Save me. You can't leave me. Help me! God! Help me!"

Longarm stood, Clarice cradled in his arms. He took one last moment to look back at Buddy Matthews sinking in a lake of fire. Then turned and raced for the stairs and the safety of the night air outside.

He got her out, out into the cool evening breeze, her charred clothing fused into her flesh. But he got her out as behind them the age-dried timbers of the old Matthews house fed an ever growing flame.

He got her out as neighbors began to see and to run, offering help and encouragement, someone among them already clanging a steel triangle to alert the volunteer fire department.

He got her out of the burning, roaring, spark-flaring blaze and he stood there in the young night with Clarice cradled in his arms, ignoring all offers of help from the neighbors.

And after a while—it might have been minutes or might as well have been hours—he relinquished his hold on her and let them lift her out of his arms.

He thought she probably died even before he got her out of the house. But he hadn't wanted to take a chance about it. He hadn't wanted to let anyone else take her from him while there was the slightest possibility that she might feel, that she might think he was abandoning her.

He, after all, was the one who'd promised to save her, dammit. He was the one.

He let someone take her finally and shook his head and wondered how he'd gone and gotten his face all wet.

Probably from the water buckets. Or sweat. Or some such thing.

Goddammit.

Watch for

LONGARM AND THE SADDLE ROCK SPOOK

203rd in the bold LONGARM series
from Jove

Coming in November!

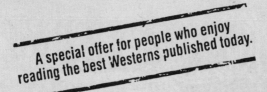